MAHOMETAN مسلمان AND CELESTIAL'S
ENCYCLOPÆDIC GUIDE TO MODERNITY

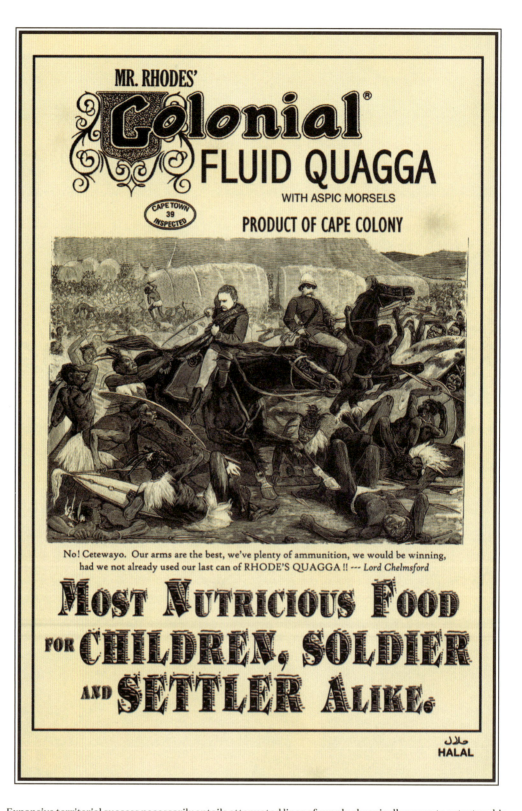

Expansive territorial success necessarily entails attenuated lines of supply chronically prone to catastrophic failure, a geostrategic irony particularly evident in the provision of perishable protein sources requisite to the sustenance of colonial presence. Attempted solutions have come in corned, tinned, liquefied and even powdered form, but have at best only temporarily ameliorated the logistical conundrum. The heavily processed comestible advertised by this promotional card exemplifies this insoluble problematic: with support from Great Britain's Colonial Office the popular demand for 'Rhovril', as it came to be known colloquially, proved so vast as to immediately outstrip supplies of the principle ingredient, rendering the product's success its own irrevocable undoing. {Similarly, cf. Liebig Company's Pulverisierte Beutelwolf-Extrakt, "The Herbertshöhe Treat®", immediately following; for a more primordial instance n.b. the enigmatic articulated nephrite megaliths revealed by recent archæological investigation to be long-abandoned Maori "presses de moa".}

USE LIEBIG "COMPANY'S" EXTRACT OF THYLACINE,

FINEST AND MOST EFFICIENT
TONIC, PURGATIVE AND RESTORATIVE FOR
MALADIES OF "THE TROPICS";

THE STRONGEST AND CHEAPEST
BECAUSE MOST CONCENTRATED:
in every strengthening sustaining 2-oz. jar the decoction of
TWO FULL THYLACINES.

WHEN BUYING ASK FOR THE
"COMPANY'S" Extract

And see that it bears the signature *J. Liebig* in BLUE ink across the Label.

DO YOU HAVE

Foreign engineers building your railroads?
Foreign bankers holding your debt?
Foreign gunboats anchoring in your harbor?

THEN YOU *NEED*

مسلمان

Mahometan
and Celestial

Chartered Purveyors of Bespoke Modernities

★ Kostantiniyye ★ Los Angeles ★ San Francisco ★ Victoria City ★

Because why be made a colony, when you can be an Empire?

Est. the 18th of October 1860

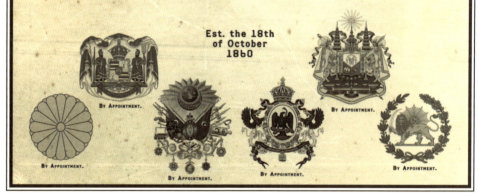

By Appointment. By Appointment. By Appointment. By Appointment. By Appointment.

Mahometan and Celestial

WANT TO "MODERNIFY" YOU
THO' IT MAY COST A TREASURY AND A HERITAGE
IT IS WORTH FAR MORE THAN BOTH.

WHY?

1st. Authoritative pronouncements and popular belief notwithstanding, we understand that this is an age of empire. "Commonwealth" is a polite euphemism for empire. "Co-prosperity sphere" is a polite euphemism for empire. "Hegemonic superpower" is a polite euphemism for empire. And "superduperpower" is an exceedingly silly euphemism for empire.

2d. An empire is not a toy. It is, however, committed to acquiring your toys, by any means necessary. Empire is a chronic militarized shopping spree, bargain hunting through superior firepower. It pays in bullets, chemical explosives, chlorine or phosgene gasses, and opium.

3d. MQ-9 Reaper is the new Gatling gun and APC-mounted water-canon the new truncheon, just as (and to ensure that) intermodal cargo container is the new amphora. Some things never change.

4th. Therefore, the only good empire is a fallen empire. But . . .

BEWARE the falling empires, as they are the worst of all, and remember: there is no shame in being made a colony, only in wishing to remain one -- do not be caught with your panung open or your sarouel down, unless you've a bowler on your head and a box cannon in your hand!

CHARTERED PURVEYORS of BESPOKE MODERNITIES,

KOSTANTINIYYE, LOS ANGELES, SAN FRANCISCO, VICTORIA CITY.

ENCYCLOPÆDIC GUIDE TO MODERNITY

Comprising a Manual of Useful Instruction

Essential to Attainment of the Urbane by the Savage, the Barbarous, and the Half-Civilized Alike

By STEVEN FLUSTY WITH PAULINE C. YU

TO THEIR
MOST IMPERIAL MAJESTIES
THESE DISCOURSES
ARE
RESPECTFULLY DEDICATED

BISMILLAH AL-BĀRI AL-MUSAWWIR

✦ To believe that the space of the nomad is smooth is to never have been a nomad ✦ The conveyance that is both viewpoint and home, the vehicle that is the einsteinian center of and perspectival lens upon landscapes urban or otherwise, cannot travel freely in all directions across deserts of sand or asphaltum ✦ No, it follows itineraries, itineraries determined by the sustenance of the transiting self, itineraries that must converge upon such stuff of life as water, food, sounds, sights, sociability, that which may prevent the body from withering to dust and the soul to shadow ✦ It is the stark protuberant contrast of such everyday stuff, the waterspouts and date palms and spires outstretched to milk the teat of God, commanded to rear up from off the vast and undistinguished plains of Id, that render even the most prosaic of things an event, a spectacle, a beckoning baited basin of attraction into which itineraries are compelled to pour, commingle and find themselves forevermore ensnared ✦ For stuff is not merely a thing but a process, the mass of stuff must necessarily wrap about itself like a patterned carpet the vast flatness of the undistinguished plains of space and time so that all else tumbles inwards, to converge and be consigned its proper place ✦ Whereas the fountain's basin sits amidst the dunebound garden to sooth and sustain the floral carpets of an imagineered paradise, so too does that basin draw those flowers up about itself from across the face of the world and stake them to an ornamental cross-axis that all the world is forced to bear ✦ And so too does its very presence command the attendance, compel the gathering and choreograph the collision of the itineraries, the conveyances, the bodies and the souls of nomads ✦

THE AUTHOR'S PREFACE TO THE VIGILANT READER:

On the Plan, Scope and Practical Application of the Work.

"Mahometan & Celestial's Encyclopædic Guide to Modernity, Comprising a Manual of Useful Instruction Essential to Attainment of the Urbane by the Savage, the Barbarous, and the Half-Civilized Alike", is an incomparable compendium of expeditionary reports, exhibited artifacts and concise aphoristic notes from the field that charts the most direct and unfailing course to the modern, meticulously presented so as to be readily comprehensible to any reader no matter how putatively backward or decadent.

It may be trusted that ours is indeed the concern best qualified to guide the reader safely along this elsewise fraught and treacherous course. Founded in response to long and widespread series of transnational unpleasantries culminating in the despoliation of Peking's summer palaces at the denouement of the Second Opium War, we at Mahometan & Celestial LLC full well understand that a process of "MODERNIFICATION™", no matter how reluctantly or cynically undertaken, is the best defense against the onslaught of any missionizing civilizade. Regrettably, perhaps, our response is roughly a century and a half belated at the very least, but do any of us truly exercise control over when happenstance inserts us into the continuum of history? Thus equipped with nearly a half century's aggregate experience in the fields of natural history and metropolitan geography, and firm in the conviction that the early 21st Century is the new late 19th, we are dedicated to the broad dissemination, to all interested at-risk parties, of instruction and observation on the

subject of conquest-avoidance by means of do-it-yourself re-civilizing, a task readily accomplished by means of careful attention to the following pages' dissections of the modern, alongside forensically annotated displays of the consequently excised relics evincing past aspirations thereto.

So, do you dread the spontaneous denial of airship passage by reason of the cut of your frock, the tone of your complexion, or the form of your orison? Fear no longer! Through assiduous application of the lessons contained within these pages, the diligent reader is categorically guaranteed to reap the benefit of metropolises and entrepôts relieved of such troublesome nuisances as foreign gunboats, financiers, missionaries, &c. At Mahometan & Celestial LLC, when we hear Great Powers invoke the shibboleth "civilization", we chamber a round in our C96 "broomhandle" Mauser. With this encyclopædic guide grasped in hand and its counsel taken to heart, so too gentle reader shall you.

TABLE OF CONTENTS

PAGE 16

Metropolographical Expeditionary Report No. 22:

The Rime of the Frequent Flyer, or, What the Elephant Has Got in His Trunk.

SPECIMENS EXPROPRIATED BY THE EXPEDITION

ENGROSSED AND ILLUMINATED NOTES FROM THE FIELD

PAGE 75

Metropolographical Expeditionary Report No. 49:

The Emperor's Dirty Laundry, or, a Tale of Seven Cities Remade to Measure.

SPECIMENS EXPROPRIATED BY THE EXPEDITION

ENGROSSED AND ILLUMINATED NOTES FROM THE FIELD

PAGE 134

Catalogue of Specimens Expropriated by Previous, Interim and Subsequent Metropolographical Expeditions.

FULLY ILLUSTRATED AND UP-TO-DATE

PAGE 189

EPILOGUE:
The Allegory of the Undisclosed Location, a Platonic Dialogue Revelatory of the Greater Circumstances Governing the Conduct of this Work.

PAGE 194

References, Sources and Acknowledgements.

PAGE 197

About the Authors.

COVER IMAGE
Depicting a coterie of modernising autocrats,
this poster {reproduced at cover's center}
by an unknown 19th Century engraver
subsequently served as unaccredited inspiration
for many a Manhattanite artiste and plagiarist.

Metropolographical Expeditionary Report No. 22

THE RIME OF THE FREQUENT FLYER

OR,

What the Elephant Has Got in His Trunk.

SUMMARY

Touring is commonly taken for the frivolous offspring of shrinking distance and expanding leisure time. The miscegenation of these very modern phenomena gives rise in turn to vast and diffuse landscapes bound together by particular tour itineraries and conveyances, anchored by tourist attractions and traps, and saturated by the effluvia from bottomless reservoirs of souvenirs. The spatially and temporally specific significances of these landscapes, however, harbor far deeper and more sordid truths awaiting excavation, and thus we here set forth to plumb those depths. In so doing, touring shall be exposed as not just an excrescence of modernity, but as culpable for the all-consuming germination of the modern and, not at all incidentally, for the production, elaboration and maintenance of the imperial along the way, leaving us perpetually lost in transit and ineluctably the tourists we strive to avoid.

KEY WORDS
conquest, Gatling gun, Looty, pachyderm, tourism, Vanderdecken

What am I missing? This is perhaps the most uncomfortably nagging question to colonize my head whenever I find myself sealed into an aluminum can and hurled across the troposphere. Wedged into four square feet of space, at most, for untold hours as I excrete my own personal quarter ton of carbon onto the world below, I find myself obsessively wondering if I remembered to lock the stove, pack the front door, and turn off my passport on the way out. I know there is something I must have forgotten, as does every other traveler shoehorned into steerage class here with me. No procession of slightly outdated movies, truncated and miniaturized to accommodate our friable sensibilities and seatback screens, can assuage the anxiety.

The question, however, is neither so simply pragmatic nor so existentially limited to the prolonged moment of transit—that homogeneous bardo of seat pitches and overhead bins suspended outside the space and time of home and destination, interrupted only by occasional bouts of turbulence that viscerally recollect the precariousness of our present disposition. Rather, I believe the question permeates touring itself. I do not mean by this to imply I have derived a single, universal explanatory algorithm of optional travel. While it is unlikely there are as many rationales for travel as there are travelers, given that persons setting out upon similar ventures must have motivations that are at least congruent to some degree, my conversations with my fellow in-seat-mates have certainly elicited a broad range of explanations for our shared confinement. Some are en route to relaxation, others to excitement, yet others to the different, to the unexpected (but not too unexpected, most—although not quite all—of us hope), to the new, or to the long lost. Such variation leads in turn to a variety of tourisms. To sun-and-cocktail-drenched tropical paradises nestled within perimeter fortifications of razor ribboned chainlink and aerosolized insecticide. To olde townes saturated with Taylorized handicrafts and tourist police. To charnel scenes of memorialized atrocities retrofitted with restrooms, snackbars, understated purveyors of mementos of mass mori, and interpretive placards thoughtfully arrayed along pedestrian paths.

But despite their diversity, a collective discomfort crosscuts the lot—we are all missing something, something we believe we must be able to find somewhere elsewhere. We pour through libraries of unceasingly updated guidebooks that instruct us where to find it. We purchase package tours that promise to lead us straight to it. It would, after all, be a shame to go all that way and somehow miss it. And whatever it is we believe we are missing, it must be something vastly important and irresistibly attractive. Otherwise why would we subject ourselves to imprisonment in four square feet of imperceptibly

A state of considerably worse repair.

yet inflammably propelled space to begin with, let alone pay for the experience?

SIGHTSEEING, OR BUT WHAT, THEN, IS IT? "Whatever it may be, ironically purpled verbiage will get you no closer to it," my traveling companion mutters condescendingly, reminding me that I have thus far missed mentioning him at all. We have traveled together off and on since I was very young, and he is prone to addressing me in this tone. It is the tone of one accustomed to authority, but also a tone I have heard gradually soured by his long years in exile following his deposition from his rightful throne. Or so he accounts for his present disposition, although he has never struck me as particularly royal in his battered derby hat and his threadbare suit faded from what must once have been a becoming shade of green. Not to mention the sizeable trunk he carries with him at all times, although this is to be expected given that he is an elephant. One might think this would strike onlookers as odd, but nobody seems to notice. In fact, nobody but I ever much acknowledges his presence at all, although this too is unsurprising—it is common practice to ignore an elephant in the room. Or, in this instance, an elephant in the Kodak Photo Spot. "If you are at a loss for just what is missing, why not try to infer it from what you are doing—and rather incessantly, I might add—to find it? Think about what you are doing."

So what am I doing? Browsing shopfronts and surveying store contents. Amassing postcards. Composing photographs of the Flavian Amphitheater (open daily from 9am, entry fee fifteen and one-half euro), of weathered triumphal arches, of more than a dozen pilfered Egyptian obelisks, of a centurion in full armor chatting on his cellphone. Enlisting others to photograph the same, but with myself included in the foreground. I protest that what I am doing is hardly representative, as my motivations for these seemingly touristic behaviors are different. I, after all, am not engaged in common tourism but in assaying commodity landscapes and gathering evidences towards learned ends. My companion is clearly unimpressed and, in a souvenir shop a mere pilum's throw further on, it becomes apparent why.

The shop consists predominantly of row upon row of waist-high bins, each displaying upright reams of antique images in heavy cardboard mattes. Many are engravings that faithfully reproduce my photographs, but in black linework on white. The amphitheater, the arches, the obelisks, pedimented temples, domed cathedrals and ruined tumuli are all there, although most admittedly in a state of considerably worse repair. And while there is not a single cellular-toting legionnaire in sight, many of the engravings include other human figures in frame, dressed in culottes and tricorne hats. They marvel and point at the landmarks and, in at least one instance, a figure even seems to be posing for a portrait sketch in front of a triumphal arch. The shop's proprietor laughingly proclaims these "snapshots before cameras", and adds that Giovanni Piranesi made his living peddling them to the Grand Tourists of England.

He then lifts additional prints, color reproductions of oil paintings, out of another bin and introduces me to those English. Depicted here by their favorite portraitist, Pompeo Batoni, they are a sumptuous lot in their satin knee-breeches and waistcoats, their velvet cloaks and fur trimmings. Young, mid-Eighteenth Century jetsetters like Charles Crowle, Richard Milles, and Gregory Page-Turner, fortunate scions of their time's most up-and-coming superpower, posed amongst what look to be personal collections of classical busts and frieze fragments, invariably with scholarly documents and books immediately at hand (Page-Turner being a particularly apt moniker under the circumstances). They seem as keen to be witnessed as world-wise as they are to witness the world, immersing themselves in ancient glory gone to ruin while immortalizing their immersion, all to show they are now equipped for the attainment of greater glory still. And they seem nearly identical in their pursuit. They are all men, all pale-complexioned, similarly and splendidly dressed, all in possession of classical artifacts. Chuck, Dick and Greg even pose identically, right hand on hip and left resting upon field notes or route maps.

My companion fixes me with a maddeningly wry stare as if to say, "looking uncomfortably familiar, are they?" I pointedly elide the barb by grabbing another print from the bin. This one is a reproduction of Johan Zoffany's Tribuna of the Uffizi, in which a veritable package tour of Georgian Era aristocrats cluster in discussion about various, predominantly nude, objets d'art in an ornate salon lined wall-to-wall with paintings. These gentlemen are older and even more sumptuous than Batoni's, my eye drawn particularly to a nobleman in a dark velvet waistcoat encrusted with ornate gold embroidery across the chest, surmounted by a bejeweled breast star and sash. A painting is being held up for display before him, with a solicitousness suggesting the art is not merely being presented for study but offered for acquisition. As with Batoni's, Zoffany's composition enlists assemblages of a Classical past to serve as a backdrop against which knowing travelers stand illuminated in the foreground, rendering them simultaneously masters of a static antiquity and its living opposite. "And the opposite of antiquity...," my companion prompts, and there is no eliding his insight no matter how maddeningly pedantic its delivery. These are paintings of tourists inventing modernity, making themselves modern by touring.

GETTING THERE, OR THE HITCHIKER'S GUIDE TO MODERNITY.

"Successful travel, after all, relies upon timeliness. If you run late you will never be where you should be when you should. You wouldn't want to be left behind, would you?" The elephant reaches into his trunk and withdraws a timetable, waving it at me to emphasize his point. The timetable is yellowed with age, depicting the route of a weekly flight from Amsterdam to Batavia—present day North Jakarta—with only a mere two dozen stops along the way. Its cover proudly announces "14,350 kilometers in 10 to 12 days", this conquest of space and time illustrated by a graphic of the Westerkerk towering high above a thatched hut nestled in the shade of coconut palms.

As we meander between the Prinzengracht and the Singelgracht, I try to focus my attention on what is immediately in front of me, and, of course, to photograph it before it recedes behind me again. I am leery of the proposition that what we now seek through travel is our own modernity. If anything, isn't touring supposed to be a respite from the mundane routinization of modern life? My eye moves from one narrowly elongated centuries-old canal house to the next, the hoist beams of their gabled rooftops reaching out above us to the waterway beyond, their windows populated by ceramic curios in blue and white, curtain lace, and in one instance a cadre of exotically ornate wooden puppets. The effect is quaint, like stepping back in time, which I reluctantly begin to acknowledge would necessarily suggest that, in relation to the concrete everyday reality I am touring, I myself must therefore be visiting from somewhere forward in time.

More improbably still, the imagery emblazoned upon my companion's timetable seems to be somehow proliferating in ever more peculiar forms along our path. It begins innocently enough, a postcard on an outdoor rack depicting the Westerkerk rising adjacent the Prinsengracht's banks. But upon closer examination this Prinsengracht proves to be thickly lined with coconut palms, flocks of parrots and pink flamingos, while tanned swimmers cavort with wildly leaping cetaceans in the canal's water. And as we proceed, similarly dissonant imagery appears wherever we look. Stamped tin novelty placards, greeting cards and posters combining mechanical conveyances with wild animals, savage people and even mythological beasts. I purchase them as we go, harvesting souvenirs on the fly, and finally pause at a brown-bar's canalside terrace for a break, a beer, and a less frenzied assessment of my acquisitions.

The very first one confirms and compounds my suspicions. A vintage advertisement for Royal Dutch Airlines, it depicts a twin propeller driven airplane, no doubt the high technology of its day, aloft above a massive Seventeenth Century sailing ship at sea, accompanied by the slogan "The flying Dutchman, FICTION becomes FACT." The juxtaposition of the antiquated and then-modern vessels in use suggests a process of progressive evolution somehow inherent to travel technology itself, a hereditary lineage of machines whereby travel makes even itself modern. And this evolution, we are instructed, is a marvelous and perhaps even miraculous thing, whereby the mythical becomes the material. At the same time, though, something feels ominously amiss. The legendary flying Dutchman, after all, is a skipper—christened Hendrik Vanderdecken in most versions of the tale—who sets out from home for the colonies (or perhaps vice-versa) but, in mid-journey, wrathfully refuses to submit to insurmountable headwinds. For this stubborn pride, he is condemned to sail forever at top speed only to remain trapped perpetually in place between home and destination, to never make landfall or even headway, plying the seas until Judgment Day. An odd mascot for an airline, and indeed I recall my long-ago hesitancy to enroll in KLM's old "Flying Dutchman" frequent flyer program for fear that it might curse me with insurmountable departure delays or, perhaps, being imprisoned forever in some transit lounge. So the celebratory advertisement seems to have inadvertently subverted itself. Or perhaps, conversely, it is onto something, although I am not yet certain what.

This thematic contrasting of modern technology above with antitheses below proves a constant in my new cache, albeit with distinct typological variations. Two old Air France advertisements, for instance, depict a god's-eye view of propeller-studded passenger liners high above an "Extreme Orient"—stylized blank landmasses from which sprout the upturned eaves of toy pagodas. Here too the modern realizes the mythological, as in one image situating the airplane in the tail of a soaring

Dissonant imagery.

phoenix. And perhaps there is some unintended ambivalence here as well, given that the life cycle of the phoenix necessitates bursting into all-consuming flame. But the principle depiction is one of sleek, silvered mobility gliding swiftly over the tans and jewel-tones of immobile edifices rooted timelessly in exotic place below.

Four additional advertisements, one each for Air France, Air Afrique, Sabena and Pan Am, invert the perspective with ground-level views, looking skyward at modernity in flight. In one of these, it is a trio of elephants grazing obliviously below. My companion harrumphs irritably at this. In another, it is West Africans staring up in astonishment, with what is evidently intended to be a shaman (although I suspect the illustrator would have been thinking something more akin to "witch doctor") raising his arms towards the plane as though welcoming a deity. In the third, there again are those same raised arms of welcoming supplication, although here they belong to a lone Bedouin beside his camel in the desert sands. And finally, Pan Am shows us a hulking passenger liner cruising above a palm-lined tropical lagoon while, in the foreground, a reclining lei-bedecked woman in a floral kikepa welcomes the arrival with a more odalisque greeting. So it is not just edifices immobilized in exotic places but their inhabitants as well. The antithesis of the aircraft aloft is no longer yesteryear's technology, but peoples depicted as living still in yesteryear and the year before that, perhaps reaching backwards unchanging through time immemorial.

Of course, those aircraft are no less inhabited than the landscapes above which they soar, as another advertisement for Air Afrique illustrates. In this one, a passenger reclines luxuriantly in a wicker chair, gazing out the window at the palms and plantation houses arrayed beneath him. His overview of this landscape is twofold, the view out the window augmented by the map of his aerial route across Africa in his hand. While he can see all below him, we can see no more of him than the pinkness of his chin and hands. His wide-brimmed pith helmet, coordinated to match his white bush jacket, conceal his face completely.

The story told collectively by my new stash of souvenirs is revelatory. It delineates a genealogy of the modern constructed by Europeans in continually accelerating conveyances situated at ever greater heights above the past. And above others perpetually mired in that past who are, at most, able to traverse it only at the speed of a camel's trot. Another route to modernity seems to be revealing itself here, but I am thrown off course by a trumpet of alarm sounding from across the table. My companion stares aghast at the tinplate printed with the pith-helmeted passenger, snatches it up with his trunk, and hurls it into the canal. "Wicked hunter," he cryptically utters a few moments later, seemingly by way of embarrassed apology.

A final pair of stamped tin placards stand out in that, unlike the other images, they place the traveler and the local in intimate contact. One bears a sepia-toned illustration for the steamship company Rotterdam Lloyd's bimonthly service between Amsterdam and Batavia. It depicts a single-funneled steamship looming over a twig-roofed sampan in the background, while in the foreground a Javanese woman kneels over a basket of fruit at the feet of a binocular-wielding European woman in tailored white traveling clothes. This self-lionizing encounter with supplicant exoticness is reinforced on the second plaque, depicting a phalanx of mustachioed men in forage caps bicycling out of a palm forest while a gaggle of barefooted Javanese villagers look on from the sidelines. When I had grabbed this particular item, I had thought it was some sort of antique advertisement for bicycles or perhaps even for an early organizer of bicycle tours, and in a way it was the latter. A closer inspection reveals the cyclists to be dressed in blue uniforms with rifles slung over their shoulders, and the accompanying text an offer of five to thirteen guilders per week for service in the Dutch Indies Legion. These cycling tourists are occupiers.

My shopping binge, it seems, has amassed a compendium of tourists making themselves modern, and tourism making the modern, by means of manufacturing contrasts. In this instance, though, modernity is attained not by contrast with "classical antiquity" but with "living tradition". This contrast is enabled by developments in logistical technology that afford tourists opportunities to sightsee others they can position within hierarchical degrees of putative barbarity or even savagery, and to proclaim themselves civilized by comparison.

This ordinal social positioning, then, depends upon mobile geographic positioning—the itineraries that relate airlines to destinations, for instance. As depicted by my souvenir reproductions, these would include Pan Am to the South Pacific, Air France to Indochina, Sabena to Sub-Saharan Africa, and of course KLM to Java. Each flag carrier to its own territorial possession, expediting administration of, and extraction from, the colonies. And tourism alike, for these are routes that clear the way for leisure travel, routes to modernity that over time intersected and entangled to weave the network of airways we travel across today. This is certainly a thing we miss, and even prefer to miss, in our travels: the awareness of their imbrications with colonial dispossession. And if this realization is what I was missing, I am already beginning to miss missing it.

But once I have recognized this has been missing, the more pervasively it presents itself, the harder it is to miss, and the less our own touristic culpability is plausibly deniable. I lift my beer for another draught, and now notice the label: a Seventeenth Century Dutch sailing ship, over the brand name "BATAVIA", and the additional note "produced by PT Delta Djakarta TBK Bekasi, Indonesia." We set off again along the waterways, past canalhouses that are no longer so quaint. Now they have become donjons for the plundered wealth of distant shores. Even the charming puppet collection in the lace-curtained window resolves into a chain-gang of acacia-wood deities and heroes abducted from wayang golek puppet theaters some 14,350 kilometers away.

Eventually we find ourselves drawn to the sheer mass of the Bushuis Library (open Monday through Friday 9:00am until 6:00pm, entry is free of charge), a brick building in the Dutch Renaissance style large enough to fill a city block entire. We are pulled through its courtyard, beneath a baroque lintel inscribed with an interlocked VOC, into what at first glance is an unassuming meeting room. A long table and a score of modest velvet-upholstered chairs cluster at one end, the white walls and exposed beam ceiling ornamented only with a gilt-garlanded and marbled fireplace set amidst a handful of framed pictures: a map or two of Asia, and paintings depicting Couchyn (now Cochin) on the Malabar Coast, Canton, and between the two the fortress of Batavia—all sites of Dutch merchant settlement. And despite the unpretentiousness of the setting, what I had been missing overwhelms me in this room that once sat at the very center of it all, the boardroom of the United East India Company. The intimate and immediate place from whence routes were

No longer so quaint.

determined, sailors hired and dispatched (from the very courtyard through which we ourselves have just passed), native populations decimated and ruling dynasties unseated half a world away, and everything from porcelain to pepper—and puppets—drawn the many thousands of miles back again.

Somewhere along our travels, seeing the world and experiencing its civilizations became stealing the world while excoriating its civilizations. Is it that travel is power, the power to be the modern, extracted from those one encounters along the way for distillation into the new, the next and the latest? Is this where tourism begins, and its infrastructure originates? If so, might this give some clue as to why the term tourist is frequently used as an obloquy?

DINING, OR EAT, PREY, LOATHE.
"Self-loathing is not particularly becoming in a tourist," my elephantine friend cautions me, "nor do I share in it. While I cannot for the life of me clearly recollect what turn of events first initiated my own travel," an assertion I find astonishing given my companion's uncanny capacity to remember absolutely everything else, "I certainly recall both its pleasures and its efficacy in readying me for my…ahem…crowning achievement. But if you are so committed to your convictions, far be it from me to blacken your soul further with any more of this!" he adds wryly, placing another square of estate-grown, single-origin chocolate into his mouth and savoring it dramatically.

We are exploring a cluster of chocolate shops (open daily 9am until 10pm, entry is free of charge but the chocolate most definitely is not) just south of the Grand Place, methodically journeying from Valrhona to Leonidas to Godiva and back again, simultaneously taking our tastebuds on tour from Madagascar to Ecuador with layovers in the Ivory Coast and Dominican Republic. Yet throughout it, I keep thinking not "chocolate" but "tchocoatl", and its violent expropriation by a typically high-spirited tour group of Spanish souvenir-hunters during their Mexican Riviera cruise's shore excursion nearly five centuries ago. My companion thinks my misgivings an unwarranted stretch, showily savoring another bite while exaggeratedly declaiming, "No, not a hint of blood, just the unadulterated flavor of fine Belgian chocolate. But if you can show otherwise then lead on, Ferguson." Noting the jesting reference, I take up the challenge. It is not far to the Cinquantenaire, (open Tuesday through Saturday from 10:00am until 5:00pm, entry fee five euro), a pleasant monument-studded formal park that at the close of the Nineteenth Century was the site of a major national exhibition. The exhibition's central venue remains to this day. Its two wings of exhibit halls embrace us expansively, terminating on either end with facades that strike me as perfect summations of modernity's geneology—classical stone temples of Doric stone columns rising from rusticated stone bases, topped with barrel vaults of industrial iron and glass, ornamented with ironwork crowns, shields, and bemedaled sashes. The two

Perfect summations of modernity.

wings are centrally conjoined by the triplicate gaping portals of a towering triumphal arch surmounted by verdigris muses, angels blowing gilt trumpets, and a militant quadriga. The arch's coffered underside is embossed repeatedly with King Leopold the Second's monogrammatic crowned double-L, the adjacent facades emblazoned with murals featuring militantly stylized soldiers on the march in steel helmets and greatcoats while goddesses and mere mortal women look on in varied states of undress.

"Kings will be kings," my companion muses sympathetically, to which I respond, "That they will, Ferguson," and request his travel copy of Mark Twain. With some surprise, he reaches into his trunk and produces a volume of the collected works. As I expected, Innocents Abroad is particularly well-worn. But I page through until I find *King Leopold's Soliloquy*, Twain's scathing critique of Leopold's rule over his personal private colony in the Congo, where (to paraphrase page eight of the second, 1905 edition) all the riches of the land were his—his solely—and gathered for him by the men, the women and the little children under compulsion of lash and bullet, fire, starvation, mutilation and the halter. How that gathering was encouraged is made plain in accompanying photographs

Larger than life, not damned likely.

and etchings of men, women and children each relieved of a hand or foot by Leopold's colonial agents. The volume even includes what could be an alternate design for the Cinquantenaire more accurately reflective of its funding: two score of thirty-five mile long radial boulevards, each lined with four hundred thousand headless skeletons chained together, converging upon a four hundred fifty foot tall pyramid of human skulls crowned at its apex with the taxidermied corpse of Leopold II himself, machete and manacles in hand. My case, however, is only half made.

A little further on, we arrive at the Royal Museum for Central Africa, previously known as the Museum of the Congo and, before that, the Palace of the Colonies (although Palace of the Colony would have been more technically correct), an Eighteenth Century French palais built outside France towards the end of the Nineteenth, contemporaneously with the Cinquantenaire. We enter past a larger-than-life size statue of a bull elephant ridden by three naked, spear-toting African hunters, eliciting from my companion a disdainful utterance of, "Not damned likely." The entrance rotunda displays gilded allegorical statues of evidently European missionaries, saints and women-at-arms providing succor and protection to African women and children. Beyond this are the exhibition rooms, featuring ritual and everyday artifacts along with taxidermied animals all taken from the Congo Free State, and innumerable stone-engraved rolls of honor and busts celebrating the explorers and officers who took from the Congo Free State. And one room concentrates entirely upon colonial industry, describing in detail the Free State's production of rubber, cotton, tobacco, coffee and, most significantly for my purposes, cocoa.

Unsurprisingly, the usual is missing from the exhibits, just as we all prefer to miss it. There is no mention of Congolese being compelled to plant, harvest and surrender cocoa, of the failure to do so in prescribed quantities costing them quite literally arms and legs, of how this provided a model of conduct for combatants throughout the region to this day, nor of how it is precisely the heritage and continued practice of such violent expropriation that affords us our own leisure, leisure travel included. But I expect my case is made nonetheless. My companion's attention, however, is too riveted elsewhere to notice. He anxiously grasps at his tusks, and I follow his aghast stare to discover that ivory, too, was one of the colony's major exports. I turn him away, only to find us confronted by a television displaying degraded black and white footage of Africans delivering their bundles of cotton, or perhaps coffee, or even cacao—the quality of the video is too poor to be certain—to a colonial agent for weighing and payment, again with no indication of the penalty for underproduction. What is clear is that the colonial agent is clad in a white bush jacket, and matching pith helmet.

Somehow, my companion avoids shattering any of the museum's contents or fixtures in his panicked stampede out the nearest rear exit. I find him in the museum's back garden, his horrified gaze transfixed by a fountain decorated with Leopold the Second's bust, three legless Congolese warriors, and the decapitated head of a bull elephant.

SHOPPING, OR BABARIC SPLENDORS. My companion remains irritable and agitated, constantly craning his massive head as though expecting to find a pith-helmeted nemesis emerging from every shadow. I wonder at what trauma might provoke this paranoia, and whether he perceives a pith helmet atop my head as well. I myself do not see any pith helmets donned in our vicinity but, then again, perhaps my perceptions are as flawed as those incapable of seeing elephants immediately before them. "You Americans never see the world's wickedness, too busy seeing yourselves and expecting the best," my companion vents. "Narcissistic optimists, thinking every voyage is one of self-discovery, everywhere you go a mirror to uncover your shining inner light. Ptah! Does it ever occur to you that mirrors can reveal things you would not care to see?" Far from disagreeing, I want to admit that seen in relation to its past, all tourism is beginning to look to me like dark tourism. But my elephant friend needs cheering, and I know how to do it. Palaces always make him feel more at home.

Fortunately, we have at least two to choose from. Entering the eldest, we pass through a high pointed-arch gateway thickly emblazoned with arabesques of flowing golden script across black stone panels, and enter the grounds of Topkapı Palace (open 9am until 7pm Wednesdays through Mondays, entry fee twenty lira plus an additional fifteen for the harem). Wide greenswards punctuated by Cypress trees and gurgling fountains alternate with labyrinths of deep colonnades, broadly projecting eaves, and pavilions tiled in ornate patterns of blue, white and gold. The interiors are similarly ornamented, frequently lined with low divans and stocked with artifacts sufficiently elaborate to be like miniaturized concentrates of the pavilions themselves. Bejeweled thrones and daggers, delicately damascened blades, even an Imperial Wardrobe displaying richly embroidered silken caftans.

I move from one garment to the next, admiring a pattern of blood red tiger stripes and leopard spots on one, silvered peacock feathers and warding eyes on another, but am brought up short upon encountering another unlike the rest. It is in midnight blue velvet, almost black, embroidered down the front and at hem and sleeves with wide bands of intertwined leafy vines in gold thread. And I am certain I have seen something very much like it already, worn by an English nobleman in Zoffany's painting of the Uffizi. Admittedly, here it is not a fitted waistcoat but a flowing caftan. Still, the resemblance is uncanny. It is labeled merely as a robe in an antique style and dated to the second quarter of the Nineteenth Century, succeeding Zoffany by roughly half a century.

In a nearby room, I encounter a deluge of this gold embroidery upon midnight blue velvet. It is a portrait gallery, lined with depictions of Ottoman Sultans more or less in chronological order of rule. Viewed one to the next it is impossible to ignore the transformation that occurs in the early Nineteenth Century, somewhere between Mustafa the Fourth and Abdülmecid the First. Voluminous robes and massive turbans give way abruptly and entirely to dark blue jackets, gold embroidered plackets and collars, shoulder boards, the glittering breast stars of imperial orders, and the simple fez.

I express my surprise at the sudden appearance of this seeming uniform to my companion, but evidently it strikes him as so commonplace that he scarcely noted it at all. "Court uniforms, embroidered coattees—the newest, the next, the latest thing. All the rage once King George the Fourth put them on all his courtiers. No point to being à la mode," he muses, "if it is the wrong mode. The wrong fine clothes, the wrong handsome hat, and you are merely barbarous, decadent, or both. Fezzes, though," he winces, "de gustibus non disputandum est. And at least it is an improvement on those outré turbans."

Rummaging about his trunk, he removes an album of what he chucklingly

The wrong mode.

terms "family photographs", and flips through it. On its very first page is a wizened and bespectacled bull elephant, resplendent in a dark blue jacket embroidered at placket and sleeves in gold and a matching, plumed cocked hat. "My closest advisor," he tells me. The next page is a photograph of a bronze complexioned man with curly black hair and muttonchops, his dark jacket spangled with a shoulder sash, lanyards, epaulets and an octet of breast stars, its collar and cuffs embroidered with gold fern and taro leaves. A cocked hat with plumes rests on a pedestal by his side. "King David Kalākaua of Hawai'i, diplomat, legal scholar, and ardent ukuleleist." A few pages further along, a double-page spread. To the left, an elderly Asian man in yet another dark, gilt-embroidered jacket, albeit worn over a panung. "King Mongkut, Rama the Fourth of Siam, and for more formal portraits he did prefer knee breaches. His son Chulalongkorn—Rama the Fifth—was more consistent," the elephant says. He points to the picture on the right of a moustached Asian man in an embroidered, bemedaled jacket and plumed pith helmet. I notice my companion retains his composure at this last, and he in turn notices my noticing. "Sometimes you must look like a hunter to evade a hunter," he mutters, although whether he is referring to Rama the Fifth or to the contents of the entire album, I am uncertain.

Exiting back the way we came, I now find myself hunting for what could be termed Imported Baroque, and notice details I had originally overlooked. Harem chambers sporting Delft tiles and crystal chandeliers; ceiling coffers painted with trompe-l'oeil bucolic scenery; stone medallions carved with a coat of arms featuring the sultan's calligraphic tughra monogram in a sunburst and crescent over an encyclopedic array of swords, spears, revolvers, cannons, military medals and battleflags, with a cornucopia, a scale and a pair of books thrown in for good measure. A sunglass-clad Janissary sets aside his walkie-talkie and briefly explains that the tughra itself was the true imperial coat of arms, but needed some radical augmentation in the late Nineteenth Century for the other European powers to make heads or tails of it. Evidently, donning the right coat and hat are necessary but not sufficient. Even then, something is missing still, there is more to the modern than just what is on one's head and chest.

"Of course there is more," the elephant tuts, "don't forget what is beneath your backside!" He turns to a sepia-toned picture of himself in the album, a much younger elephant in a flawless derby and crisp new suit, posed in an ornate straight-backed chair atop an expensive carpet. I page through the album again and see what is pointedly, even strategically missing: there is not a divan in sight. In every picture, the assertively modern monarchs are seated on finely carved and upholstered formal chairs atop fine carpets, or standing beside more-or-less Empire style sidetables that seem to have been the universally preferred receptacle for cocked hats. Even the monarchs' poses are similar, the slightly casual lean to one side, left hand resting lightly on sword-hilt, and familiar as well. They are roughly the same postures as Messrs. Crowle, Milles, and Page-Turner.

I flippantly ask my companion if his "family" was much for traveling, and elicit an enthusiastic, "Of course, commonly preceded by these very photographs as a kind of calling card." My companion proceeds to a list of tour itineraries: Sultan Abdülaziz, the first sultan to leave the empire in peacetime, from Istanbul to Paris and London, where he received the Order of the Garter from Queen Victoria herself. King David Kalākaua, first monarch to circumnavigate the globe, from Honolulu to San Francisco and from there back due west around the world by sail and rail, meeting with his fellow kings, queens, popes, Kaisers, emperors and presidents en route. Rama the Fifth, the Royal Buddha and Great Beloved King, throughout Southeast Asia in his youth and, upon ascension to the throne, from Bangkok to London. Every stop along his way was simultaneously a major media event and a coming-out party. And while his father never made the trip, Rama the Fourth did beat a path by sending a Grand Embassy—although grand package tour seems an equally apt descriptor—of two dozen nobles and attendants to Queen Victoria's court, to spend an entire winter shivering in their tropical silks.

"And speaking of Grand Embassies, let us not forget the one Peter the Great accompanied incognito from Muscovy a century and a half earlier," the elephant concludes. "Although I suspect the true identity of a six-foot four-inch Russian autocrat calling himself Piotr Mikhaelovich was never much in doubt." Recollecting my history, it occurs to me that Peter the Great also returned to update his court by compelling them to shave off their beards, over a century and a quarter before George the Fourth would update his own by compelling them to don embroidered coattees.

So is it a universal predilection of elites everywhere, touring to make themselves modern and to make the modern along the way? And to display their modernity, and the authority it confers, for approbation both abroad and back home? Perhaps, but there are evident differences as well. For the Grand Tourist, modernity seems to be acquired through contrast with the putatively antiquated and the exotic. But for what might be termed the Grand Ambassadors, it seems to derive more from breaking with ascriptions of antiquatedness and exoticness so as to erase the contrast, from basking (and being seen to bask) not in the rusticated ruins of ancient glories but in the precision-engineered and well-oiled machinery of their contemporary analogs.

But does not that latter entail conforming to the self-serving normative standards of another, and to spoiling one's own uniqueness in the bargain? Do entire traditions go missing in the process? These misgivings arise as we make our way through the chambers of Topkapı's mid-Nineteenth Century replacement, Dolmabahçe Palace (open 9:00 am to 4:00pm Tuesday, Wednesday, and Friday through Sunday,

The latest thing.

entry fee fifteen lira plus an additional ten for the harem and a further seven for photography), a relentless pastiche of broken pediments and Corinthian columns, spiraled corbels and stone garlands, polychrome marble inlays and gold leaf accents. The cavernous interiors are precisely the sorts of parlors in which my companion's family photos must have been posed. They rooms are liberally studded with Louis XIV furniture and fittings, the world's largest Bohemian crystal chandelier, and a central staircase with banister spindles made entirely of Baccarat crystal. Were it not for the occasional inlaid tughra or gold leafed globe surmounted by a crescent moon and star, it would be difficult to determine just where in the world this palace is located. Even the mosques adjacent are concatenations of the Neoclassical, the Baroque and the Romanesque, marbled walls and trompe-l'oeil ceilings all outlined in gilt.

I find my companion in a nearby giftshop, sampling the tracks on a compact disc of Ottoman classical music from the period. Like the palace itself, they are European compositions with nods to local idioms — sonatas, fugues, marches and even a 'national' hymn composed with a surfeit of minor chords by palace conductors Giuseppe Donizetti and Callisto Guatelli, both Italian imports, both created pashas by their respective sultans. I sample a disc or two myself, Janissary mehter marches remixed as electronica, before expressing my misgivings. My companion bristles. "Remind me not to take you to Peterhof, let alone the Bang Pa In Summer Palace—you'd hate what Chulalongkorn did with the place. Or to 'Iolani Palace, you would no doubt find Kalākaua's all-night electrically-lit après surf poker parties dreadfully inauthentic. Why should you be the only ones 'spoiled' by broad streets, automobiles and busses, and fine clothes? You are somehow entitled to cocoa and ivory, but Peter the Great has no business with tooth-keys and wrung staffs? King Mongkut's emissaries must not be allowed to contaminate themselves with whatever..." and here, he fumbles in his trunk for an antique intelligence report to Her Britannic Majesty from the Siamese Grand Embassy's British handler, "'they can...thoroughly understand without the assistance of Europeans to work them... portable machines of all kinds... scientific instruments...chronometers...and arms from the best makers and of the latest improvements'?"

The act of sifting quotations calms him somewhat, but still he adds, "You may carry home anything we produce that strikes your fancy, but we are forbidden to return the favor? Would you prefer me a naked little calf riding his mother's back forever? And while we are on it," he concludes, taking on a tone of understated mischievousness, "just how are those Twenty-first Century electro-meheter remixes you have there any less tainted than their Nineteenth Century Italo-Ottoman precursors?"

ACCOMMODATIONS, OR MY PLENIPOTENTIARIES WENT TO THE CONTINENT AND ALL I GOT WAS THIS LOUSY EMBROIDERED COATTEE.

By what criteria is authenticity to be measured, I wonder, as we arrive at the doorstep of Sirkeci railway station. Which is more authentic, the imported Baroquerie of Dolmahbaçe, envisioned and realized by a loyal Ottoman-Armenian subject of Sultan Abdülmecid the First, or this very station, its Orientalist archways and Byzantine crenellations designed and financed by imported German agents of Kaiser Wilhelm the Second? And by what standard, and by whom, can such innovation be declared innocuous and even inherent to the authenticity of one civilization, but poisonous to that of another?

My companion and I board the Orient Express, yet another Belgian venture from the time of King Leopold the Second, and take our seats. All the while the elephant regales me with how a modern, civilized demeanor is not merely a matter of putting the right thing on your head, your chest, or beneath your backside, not just the parlor in which they are arrayed nor the palace that contains them all. "The sovereign traverses the broad streets no less than his subjects, his modernization is his people's." He

A learning curve so steeply surmounted.

invokes another long list of examples, proceeding from the same railway we are riding to those King Rama the Fifth stretched out from his numerous new German- and Italian-built palaces in Bangkok; expanding to include streetlight electrification and hydroelectric dams; reaching a crescendo with the construction from scratch of Saint Petersburg and, "my own lakeside capital—admirable, practical and convenient—to each elephant his own house, employment from the Bureau of Industry, and entertainment at the Amusement Hall! If one is going to undertake a Grand Embassy, after all, one may as well make the most of it."

The elephant reopens his family album towards the back, to a pair of group photos. One, labeled "First European Mission, 1862" (followed by a handwritten notation "first in centuries, anyway"), shows a party of nine well dressed gentleman immediately prior to their departure for an official state tour through Europe. They are resplendent in kimono and hakama, top knots carefully coifed and katana at hand. The other, labeled "Iwakura Mission, 1871", depicts a second party of gentlemen to tour Europe, along with much of the rest of the world, in an official state capacity. Of the party's five members, all but one are clad in fine black suit jackets and trousers, their hair parted to one side and slicked back, and all five carry top hats.

I am taken aback at such vivid evidence of a learning curve so steeply surmounted, to which my companion responds I am in good company—that of the Iwakura Mission itself. "They were just as startled to discover that their hosts were themselves parvenus although, being gentlemen, the ambassadors kept the observation to themselves." Or, more correctly, kept the observation to the pages of their diarist Kunitake Kumio's illustrated travel journal, a copy of which the elephant withdraws from his trunk to recite:

> Most of the countries in Europe shine with the light of civilization and abound in wealth and power. Their trade is prosperous, their technology is superior, and they greatly enjoy the pleasures and comforts of life. When one observes such conditions, one is apt to think these countries have always been like this, but this is not the case — the wealth and prosperity one sees now in Europe dates to an appreciable degree from the period after 1800. It has taken scarcely forty years to produce such conditions…How different the Europe of today is from the Europe of forty years ago can be imagined easily. There were no trains running on the land; there were no steamships operating on the water. There was no transmission of news by telegraph.

"And there is some cause to suspect this mission knew it was not alone in the realization, either," the elephant adds, paging through the journal to Kunitake's carefully drafted illustration of the "Bronze Horseman", the equestrian statue of Peter the Great at the center of Saint Petersburg.

My companion then returns to his family album, and points at what I take to be an example of the learning curve's summit attained—another pair of photographs. To the left, an intensely civilized young adolescent in a capacious raifuku robe and tied-on skullcap with a crest nearly half as tall as the wearer, seated on a low dais atop a tatami-covered floor. And to the right the same refined adolescent, but now sporting the beginnings of a beard and moustache, dressed in a jacket encrusted with golden embroidery at the sleeves, hem, chest and collar (although, in all fairness, the embroidered patterns are in relatively Asiatic motifs). At his elbow is a sidetable bearing a cocked hat with plumes, and he sits in an overstuffed armchair with a thickly patterned carpet beneath. "The Emperor Mutsuhito, Meiji the Great", the elephant announces, "before, after. No point to being civilized if it is the wrong civilization."

We disembark at the old Shimbashi railway station, designed in the Neoclassical style by an American and built at the last quarter of the Eighteenth Century by otherwise underemployed samurai on the brink of seeing their caste abolished entirely. Our arrival is no mean feat given that the train tracks would run directly into the sheer glass face of an adjacent highrise, were it not for the fact that while there is an arrival platform there are no tracks whatsoever. But then again, the Orient Express only ever traveled due westward from Sirkeci to Paris Gare de l'Est in the first place, rendering the Orient itself no less a mobile absurdity.

As is to be expected at any railway station, this one has a rack of postcards to facilitate tourists' reportage of their travels to audiences back home. And as might be expected of any reconstructed late Nineteenth Century railway station, were such a station to be expected at all, these postcards replicate imagery of the period. Being less expensive in bulk, I purchase a packet assortment of them, and flip through them as we walk.

Together, the postcards constitute something of a pictorial inventory of the souvenirs returned home by the missions. The topmost card in the stack depicts the station itself, with a topknotted engineer piloting his train towards awaiting passengers in kimonos. The next shows a quartet of affluent women by a lakeside, dressed in a mixture of kimonos and Victorian ruffled gowns, a woman in the foreground working a hand-powered sewing machine. A third displays a unique hybrid image—a graphic of a hand-cranked telephone atop a sidetable cloaked in a richly embroidered cloth, adjacent an inset roundel ornamented with cherry blossoms containing an early black and white photograph of switchboard operators lined up at their stations. Another portrays a cadre of imperial dignitaries in a profusion of dark jackets, gold filigreed chests and cuffs, epaulettes, cocked hats, and tall straight-backed chairs. There is also a profusion of moustaches, luxuriant beards, and one truly prodigious pair of muttonchops—no mean accomplishment for a gentleman of Japan—and I cannot help but wonder which are more modern, Peter the Great's forcibly clean-shaven courtiers or the Meiji Emperor's conscientiously bewhiskered counterparts.

The packet includes a card bearing a portrait of the imperial family itself, the bearded Emperor Meiji in dark coat with gold embroidery and braid, his Empress in damasked Victorian gown, with the heir apparent between them in miniaturized black naval livery with brass buttons. They sit in upholstered gold-framed armchairs with a potted bouquet of chrysanthemums between them, a golden screen depicting pine forests and Mount Fuji as the background. In its poses and furnishings, this imperial portrait strikes me as familiar. It seems a variant on one in my companion's album, of Rama the Fifth in his parlor with his Regent Queen and their five royal offspring, some of whom are also dressed in scaled-down sailor suits. That latter portrait, however, is most telling for what it does not depict of the family—Rama V's three other queens, twenty consorts, and seventy-two additional children. This portrait, conversely, is more telling in the technique it uses to depict the Meiji Emperor's family—by means of the centuries-old technology of polychrome woodblock printing. In fact, all these picture postcards of newly imported mechanical, sartorial and administrative technologies are produced with the same, centuries-old technique, perhaps as a means of rendering their depicted topics more apprehensible for the audiences of their time.

At the same time, the audience's apprehension is depicted as well. A postcard accredited on its back to Utagawa Yoshifuji and entitled *Imported and Japanese Goods: Comic Picture of a Playful Contest of Utensils*, envisions two armies locked in combat. One consists of kimono-clad paper lanterns, palanquins, bamboo-ribbed wagasa parasols and stacks of woodblock prints. The other is comprised of kerosene lamps, rickshaws and steam locomotive engines, umbrellas and framed photographs, all dressed in trousers and red military jackets. The latter army appears to be winning. My companion and I pause at what may as well be the site of this battle, a bridge over the Nihonbashi River that constitutes the center of the country entire—the zero-mile from which all distances are measured. This bridge's wide, graceful wooden arch can be found in numerous Hiroshige woodblock prints. It can not, however, be found spanning the river. In its place, we come upon a low Neoclassical double archway of stone, rusticated at its base, supporting a flat asphalt causeway with wide balustered side rails. Along these rails are patinated cast metal lamp stanchions conjoined to sculptures of guardian lions and dragons realized in muscularly realist Victorian idiom. Or perhaps more correctly, muscularly realist Wilhelmite as the architect, Tsumaki Yorinaka, had brought this latest style back with him from his extended stay in Berlin. And more completely, Wilhelmite except insofar as the lamps are translations of paper lanterns into metal, the dragons seemingly crossbred between European and East Asian stock, and the lions more akin to what one

The form of modernity accomplished.

might find in front of a Chinese temple than at the foot of the Nelson Column.

The triumph of this early Nineteenth Century viaduct over its early Seventeenth Century predecessor, however, is itself contested. The bridge and its protective beasts now lurk in shadows cast perpetually by the stripped-down concrete columns and steel beams of a multi-lane overhead expressway. This more recent battle between the new and the newer for the country's zero-mile, however, has not extirpated the original wooden bridge entirely. Its replica can be visited inside a museum some distance removed.

I ponder, with sharpening sardonicism, whether this is the form of modernity accomplished. The elephant hands me a stack of brittle newspaper clippings in silent answer, along with his collected Mark Twain opened towards the middle of *Innocents Abroad*. The top clipping is a yellowed copy of October 23rd, 1872's *Newcastle Daily Chronicle,* reporting disappointment with the Iwakura Mission: "[t]he gentlemen were attired in ordinary morning costume and except for their complexion and the oriental cast of their features, they could scarcely be distinguished from their English companions." But attached to this clipping is an editorial cartoon from a German newspaper of the period, captioned, "the Japanese, true to their mission of becoming familiar with European culture, get themselves an inside view in Essen", and depicting caricatures of grinning, top-knotted samurai sticking their heads into the breech of a giant Krupp field cannon.

Nor, apparently, were the Japanese the only ones trapped between the rock of disappointment and the hard place of disparagement. Another clipping, from June 19th, 1867's *Le Figaro*, acknowledges popular regrets over Sultan Abdülaziz' European enough appearance despite his red fez: "without doubt, not as marvelous as we believed…". Conversely, upon seeing the Sultan in Paris during his own Grand Tour, Twain describes him as "stout, dark, black bearded, black eyed, stupid, unprepossessing", and reported:

> Napoleon III, the representative of the highest modern civilization, progress and refinement; Abdul Aziz, the representative of a people by nature and training filthy, brutish, ignorant, unprogressive, superstitious — and a government whose Three Graces are Tyranny, Rapacity, Blood. Here in brilliant Paris, under this majestic Arch of Triumph, the first century greets the nineteenth!

Critics of colonialism, it seems, are not immune to thinking like colonizers themselves. "Typically American, that. Like Niebuhr said, frantically avoiding recognition of one's own imperial impulses, all the while turning Kalākaua into a figurehead and using the price tag for his modern palace as an excuse to do it!" the elephant snorts. "Gone too far while somehow never having gone far enough, in the end you are still just a pachyderm in a suit, no matter how artfully embroidered your court uniforms, how opulent your palace, how many

Bureaus of Industry and Amusement Halls you build, or how grandly you tour the crowned heads of Europe. And when they have emptied your treasury to pay for palaces and railroads, or they have discovered you have more bauxite than you are willing to surrender..." he trails off bitterly.

IN CASE OF EMERGENCY, OR AM I MODERN ENOUGH FOR YOU?

Noting me distracted by the prospect that no amount of mileage accrued or souvenirs amassed can ever acquire respect, my companion repeats the question: "I said, 'Am I modern enough for you *now*?'" I turn to find him posed like a hunter atop a trophy kill, a massive and wicked-looking assemblage of tubes and gears held crosswise in mock heroism across his torso. How he fit an entire Gatling gun into his trunk is beyond me, let alone how he has managed to carry it about unhindered. But of course, why would an elephant in the room suddenly attract notice merely because that room happens to contain a security checkpoint? "Upwards of four hundred rounds per minute at the mere turn of a handle can persuade even the most reluctant host to welcome you with open—or at least raised—arms. But relax," he chuckles, "nobody besides you egalitarian Americans would be so ungentlemanly as to use one of these on anything but lesser peoples. At least not before the Great War, at any rate. A good reason to never be lesser, no? Sometimes it is not enough to look the wicked hunter. Sometimes, you must become the hunter."

"Remember," he adds, "those Siamese ambassadors went shopping for more than just chronometers and scientific instruments." Returning to his family album, the elephant turns towards the back and indicates paired photographs of rakish soldiers. One wears a fez and prodigious beard, but also a thickly bemedaled Imperial German dress uniform. The other is clean-shaven and young, a Blue Max and Iron Cross prominent upon his feldgrau dress tunic, all topped off by a tall lamb's wool kalpak hat emblazoned with a dramatically winged crescent moon. My companion makes the usual introductions, "Gifts from the Kaiser: The Baron Bodo-Borries von Ditfurth, sent to reorganize the Ottoman army; Hauptmann Hans-Joachim Buddecke, an aerial ace to the Sultan." Apparently, the sultans ultimately took to complementing their Italian composers with Prussian tacticians.

Flipping through the last of my postcard pack, it becomes apparent the sultans weren't alone in this. The final card of the set, accredited as Toyohara Chikanobu's *Observance by His Imperial Majesty of the Military Maneuvers of Combined Army and Navy Forces*, displays a woodblock print of exactly that. The Meiji Emperor stands high atop a hill, field glasses in hand, while below him soldiers and sailors clad in uniforms crossbred from French and American acquisitions practice Prussian battlefield tactics with ordnance brought from Britain. "There is, in theory, no evident reason that colonies should be reserved for the itineraries of

Grand Tourists, or that extracts of colonies should power the West alone with the new, the next and the latest," my companion observes. In response, I note that theory is not practice, nor necessarily lived experience. "You have heard of the Treaty of Sèvres, have you not? Or of Hiroshima and Nagasaki?" my companion mutters in agreement, disconsolately.

Unsurprisingly enough, my companion now suggests that another palace tour will do us good. The degree to which this predilection has begun manifesting as an obsession at times of unsettlement concerns me. I suppose, however, that it is to be expected in my present company, given what it is that a deposed monarch must be most inclined to miss. So I accompany him to the Yuanmingyuan, the Old Summer Palace (open daily 7:00am to 5:30pm winter, 7:00am to 7:00pm summer, entry fee ten yuan, plus an additional fifteen for the concessions). The Yuanmingyuan is less a palace, though, than a deluxe resort for rulers. It is an eight hundred and sixty acre conurbation of palaces, pavilions, undulating colonnades and shaded courtyards clustered around innumerable artificial lakes and canals. My elephantine fellow traveler waxes poetic about the site:

> Build a dream with marble, jade, bronze and porcelain, frame it with cedar wood, cover it with precious stones, drape it with silk, make it here a sanctuary, there a harem, elsewhere a citadel, put gods there, and monsters, varnish it, enamel it, gild it, paint it, have architects who are poets build the thousand and one dreams of the thousand and one nights, add gardens, basins, gushing water and foam, swans, ibis, peacocks, suppose in a word a sort of dazzling cavern of human fantasy with the face of a temple and palace.

Although he does then admit, with some slight embarrassment, that the description is not his own. Withdrawing a tied sheaf of correspondence from his trunk, he rifles through it until he finds the excerpt, in a letter signed by no less a personage than Victor Hugo himself.

Regrettably, though, we seem to have missed the place, and done so by a century and a half. Instead, we find ourselves standing amidst a vast plain of ruins strewn out in every direction as far as the eye can see. Empty foundations and vast piles of broken stone, punctuated intermittently by a crumbling moon bridge or partially effaced and toppled frieze, rim the banks of reedy lakes and eroded canals. Further along, we encounter a dense cluster of shattered monoliths like the wreckage of catastrophic collision between Chinese and Enlightenment-era European manor houses traveling at high speeds, a gigantic graveyard of Chinoiserie. Baroque pilasters and rococo columns with complexly faceted moldings jut up into the bare air in support of nothing, ornately medallioned porticoes topped by curlicued pediments grant entry to emptiness, long dry fountain basins in the form of massive stone seashells project from desiccated rubble.

As the occasional carved stone interpretive placard makes clear, in Chinese

A good reason to never be lesser.

and intermittently idiosyncratic English, this is what one gets when one hesitates to receive repayment in opium from a well-armed debtor. My companion expands upon the story, paging through his sheaf of correspondence to locate a letter home from Charles Gordon (late of Khartoum), one of the 3,500 soldiers who spent a full two days looting the place and another two setting much of it ablaze:

> We…went out, and, after pillaging it, burned the whole place, destroying in a Vandal-like manner most valuable property which would not be replaced for four millions. We got upwards of £48 a-piece prize money before we went out here; and although I have not as much as many, I have done well…[y]ou can scarcely imagine the beauty and magnificence of the places we burnt. It made one's heart sore to burn them; in fact, these palaces were so large, and we were so pressed for time, that we could not plunder them carefully. Quantities of gold ornaments were burnt, considered as brass. It was wretchedly demoralising work for an army. Everybody was wild for plunder.

I am reminded of a t-shirt I encountered at a pirate supply store on a previous excursion, emblazoned with the slogan "pillage before plunder, what a blunder; plunder before pillage, mission fulfillage." In the same spirit, I find myself ruefully redacting the platitudes of ethical tourism into more historically accurate formulations along the lines of "take only valuables, leave only ruins."

Delving deeper into my companion's letters, we discover these sentiments stirred in us by the surrounding devastation are not ours alone. Victor Hugo's own narration of the palace continues:

> One day two bandits entered the Summer Palace. One plundered, the other burned… [t]he devastation of the Summer Palace was accomplished by the two victors acting jointly. Mixed up in all this is the name of Elgin, which inevitably calls to mind the Parthenon. What was done to the Parthenon was done to the Summer Palace, more thoroughly and better, so that nothing of it should be left. All the treasures of all our cathedrals put together could not equal this formidable and splendid museum of the Orient. It contained not only masterpieces of art, but masses of jewelry. What a great exploit, what a windfall! One of the two victors filled his pockets; when the other saw this he filled his coffers. And back they came to Europe, arm in arm, laughing away. Such is the story of the two bandits…[b]efore history, one of the two bandits will be called France; the other will be called England.

Little wonder, then, that my companion and I find little by way of souvenirs. And as per Hugo's commentary, ultimate responsibility for this must rest with Lord James Bruce, the Eighth Earl Elgin, successor to his father Lord Thomas Bruce. Lord Thomas, one-time ambassador to Ottoman Sultan Selim the Third, is best known for his thorough tour of the Athenian Acropolis, pieces of which returned with him as souvenirs he had gotten for a steal. His son's latter scorched-earth shopping spree was similarly prodigious, yielding bejeweled and silken giftware for friends in high places back home: gigantic cloisonné vases, gilded jade scepters, richly embroidered imperial robes, elaborately carved thrones, even the first Pekingese ever to be seen in Europe—christened by Queen Victoria with the jocularly shameless name of Looty. Additional to this transfer of imperial regalia, bronze fountainheads wrought in the form of zodiacal animals seem to have been particularly hot commodities, periodically turning up to this day for auction at Sotheby's and Christie's. Postcards excepted, reproductions of these decapitated fountainheads in materials ranging from cold cast resin to verdigris bronze are the only keepsakes we find on offer in the interpretive center's giftshop, available in various sizes and assorted price levels. Perusing the shelves with my companion, I give silent thanks that the animals of the Chinese zodiac do not include the elephant.

Simultaneously perusing the elephant's collection of correspondence, however, we are startled to discover that the disgust we share with Victor Hugo over this triumphalist thievery is reiterated by none other than Lord James himself. We pour over dispatch after dispatch, and in each the Eighth Earl Elgin excoriates his empire's machinations, his fellow subjects for demanding them, his soldiers for executing them, and himself for commanding them. As to the Yuanmingyuan specifically, he writes:

> I have just returned from the Summer Palace. It is really a fine thing, like an English park—numberless buildings with handsome rooms, and filled with Chinese curios, and handsome clocks, bronzes, &c. But, alas! Such a scene of desolation…There was not a room I saw in which half the things had not been taken away or broken in pieces…Plundering and devastating a place like this is bad enough, but what is much worse is the waste and breakage.…War is a hateful business. The more one sees of it, the more one detests it.

Yet, to use an Orwellian turn of phrase, he went ahead and did it just the same.

If the Yuangmingyuan embodies the tourist's ultimate nightmare, destinations entirely despoiled through ravenous acquisition, then Lord James in turn is both the prototype and the paradigm of the tourist's self-loathing: the cultural tourists revulsed by the impact of their own presence upon the peoples they tour, the ecotourists lamenting their own swelling carbon footprints midflight. Indeed, all of us who in our travels strain to think of others as tourists but not ourselves, to revile their presence alongside our own and to avoid their "tourist spaces."

All the while, we continue in our travels to avail ourselves of the acquisitions some very indelicate souvenir hunters brought back in their baggage, and the routes they established to make good their escapes. Our travels, then, are inextricably rooted in conquest, concealed beneath the traveling cloak of the new, the next, the latest, in short—the modern. Vaguely suspecting this and repressing those suspicions, we nurture our contempt for the tourist who somehow is not, must not be, could not be us. It is the assiduously ignored elephant we prefer to miss that nonetheless accompanies us in our travels.

But it is just one in a herd of like absences, a grand ambassador for the willfully unseen pachyderm at the heart of the modern that manifests simultaneously within our own hearts as well. It is our inner king of all elephants, forever afraid of being a pretender to the throne of the now and constantly in danger of being dethroned by change. We are naggingly colonized by the constant absence of we don't and can't know what, an insatiable hunger for whatever is newer and next and so does not even exist yet to be had, conjoined to the absence of what we continually surrender to attain what is always just beyond reach. So of course something is missing, and of course we can never apprehend what it is.

We have become the fiction of the flying Dutchman made fact, all members of Vanderdecken's crew. Whether we signed on voluntarily or found ourselves impressed by force, we are all sailors for a global imperium of discontent. The pasts we could never have experienced irrevocably rendered and mummified as picturesque ruins and tourist attractions, the future fated to become the claustrophobic and inadequate present at every moment of arrival, our souvenirs melting into air within our grasp. Our perpetual travel in pursuit of what will always necessarily be missing dooms us to sail with all our might merely to remain in place, to stave off being blown backwards and left behind, as the tantalizingly new becomes the intolerable now.

If we can make no headway, why undertake the voyage to begin with? True, there are some exquisite souvenirs to be netted along the way. But over the course of my own travels, I believe my companion has provided me the answer we have been missing. Just as travel gives rise to the modern, the modern's travels time and again give rise to an indisputable object lesson: those who do not subject themselves to modernity's relentless and shifting winds are forever in danger of finding themselves subject to those who have.

Thus are we all, all who can afford the luxury anyway, pulling geographics as the recovering addicts call it, and playing Elgin all the while. Traveling from place to place in acquisitive search of idyllic paradises, unspoiled cultures, shining paragons of luxuriant technological utopias or vicarious encounters with brutal mass mortalities past or ongoing. We transit through endless chains of departure lounges and arrival gates, passenger cabins and hotel lobbies, never to find rest until we have attained the irremediably unattainable.

Metropolographical Expeditionary Report No. 22

SPECIMENS

EXPROPRIATED

BY THE

EXPEDITION

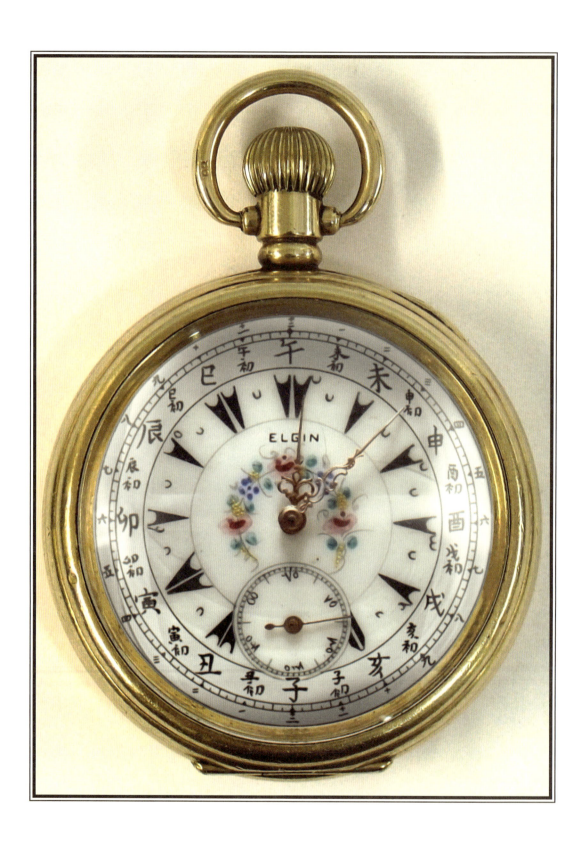

Based upon an appropriated Southwest Roumelian horologe amalgamated with a clepsydra annexed from Tien-Tsin, this dual-purpose klopechronograph and chronoleilameter by the noted watchmakers {and procurists of contestably derived artifacts} Elgin & Son remains indispensible to any and all conducting extralegal salvage missions across time zones and culture circles.

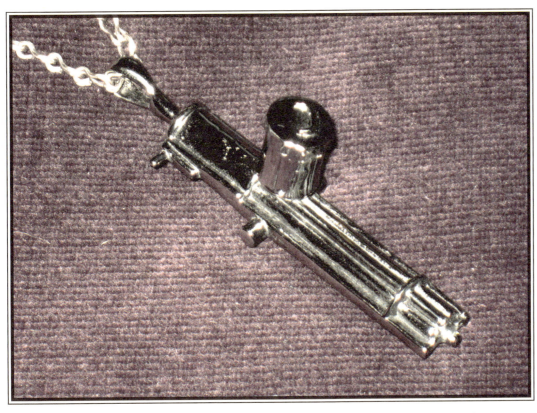

Typical of devotional jewelry worn by congregants of the Heterodox Church of the Tropics, this amulet venerates "the uncounted and uncountable martyrs who died at a distance of two thousand yards for our sins."

Trade cards such as those here displayed served to promote chocolate manufactured from only the finest cocoa to be found anywhere in the Congo Free State {État indépendant du Congo}, with this particular voluminous series of cards taking as its theme the genesis of chocolate itself, from plantations far distant to the arcade storefront of one's own neighborhood chocolatier.

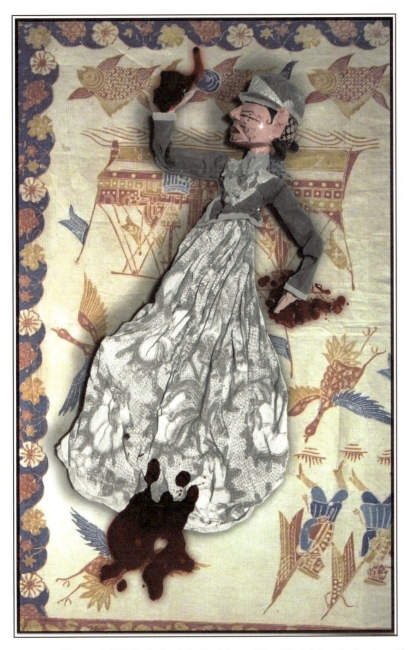

As the tightening grip of the Koninklijk Nederlands Indisch Leger {Royal Dutch East Indies Army} battered the Javanese with fusillades of phonographic recordings and kinetoscopic pictures, it became evident to even the most hard-bitten puppeteer that the fall of the island's venerable wayang golek theaters was both ineluctable and imminent. Thus, upon finding themselves finally surrounded by enemy gramophones and kinetographs loaded and aimed, the wayang elected to mount a final performance of suicidal resistance. Costumed in funerary white and armed with miniature krisses, they took the stage and, to the invading audience's confused horror, set to lethally severing one another's cempurits {arm rods} and penudings {torso handles}. The mortal remains of this paroxysmic 'puppetan', including the ensanguined wayang here displayed, were in turn ceremonially immolated by their dalangs, who in many instances accompanied their creations into the flames.

To underscore the literal implementation of wakon-yōsai {和魂洋才, roughly translatable as "Japanese spirit, Western techne"} in the presence of the Emperor himself, the Kunai-shō {Imperial Household Ministry} took charge of repopulating the palace precincts with only the most up-to-date of domesticated tsukumogami {tool-spirits}. While objects of everyday use naturally acquire souls only after the passage of a full century, the Kunai-shō succeeded in adapting the latest imported technologies so as to condense the process into a few short weeks. This ambrotype depicts one such resultant imperial tsukumogami, a shinchōchinobake {new-lantern-ghost} availing itself of a rare solitary moment to pay respects to its inanimate ancestors.

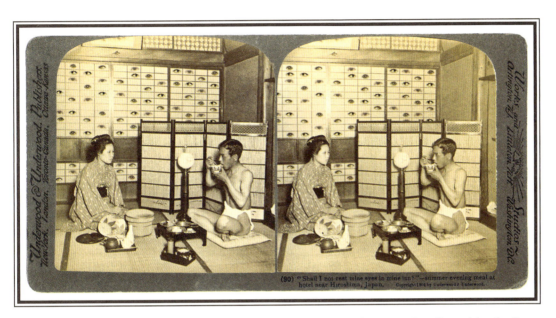

Such enlisted tsukumogami proved a similarly potent means to secure the restoration of imperial authority beyond the palace grounds, as with the tennōnomokumokuren {heavenly-sovereign's-lord-many-eyes} here so engrossed in the act of domestic intelligence gathering as to have overlooked the stereographer entirely. Created as a less unsavory replacement for outcaste okappiki police informants, tennōnomokumokuren were particularly adept at scoping out homegrown malcontents and seditionists.

Entitled "Geleneklerin İhaneti" {"The Treachery of Traditions"}, painter Mustapha Kemal Pasha created this work during his Republican Period in response to the lingering horrors of the Great War. Although highly influential in both the artistic and sartorial arenas, this piece's impact upon the latter proved less than salubrious with the subsequent discovery that, when confronted by such mishaps as a sudden steam-boiler failure, goggles are far more difficult to lower in a timely fashion from above the brim of a top hat, bowler or homburg.

Metropolographical Expeditionary Report No. 22

ENGROSSED

&

Illuminated

NOTES FROM THE FIELD

With the locals either dead or refugees, there remained no one but the soldiers to purchase the rugs. And so they wove their paisleys into antipersonnel devices, and their hound's-tooths into hand grenades.

Confronted with the growing instability of Tsar Nicholas the Second's regime, Minister of the Interior Vyacheslav von Plehve reportedly suggested, "We need a small victorious war to stem the tide of revolution" (Witte, as quoted in Dallin, 1950, p. 90). Ultimately the war proved to be neither small nor victorious, giving rise to mass desertions, widespread urban unrest, internecine intra-court murderous assassinations, insoluble legitimacy crises and, finally, regicide followed by a protracted civil war. Historians have since suggested that von Plehve's proposal, assuming it was made at all, was done so in jest. All of which serves to underscore the popular maxim, "it is the thought that counts."

> We had to destroy the global village in order to save it.

The weed of nationality must be refreshed, from time to time, with the blood of aliens and outcasts.

𒀭 𒁹 𒈨 ˄ 𒈨𒌑 𒍝 𒃻
𒅆 ˄ 𒁹𒌨𒂊 𒅆 ˄ 𒈨𒌑 𒍝 𒃻
𒈨𒌑 𒅗 𒀭 𒈨𒌑 from deep in the heartlands of three dozen countries the seeds should have yielded exportable broccoli Xerox machines ˄ Instead, all that came up was salt, and debt 𒈨𒌑 𒍝 𒃻 𒈨𒌑 𒅗 𒀭 𒃻 𒁹𒌨 𒃻 𒁹 ˄ 𒈨𒌑 𒍝 𒃻 𒅆 𒈨𒌑 𒅗 𒀭 ˄ 𒀭 𒁹 𒈨 𒁽 𒅗𒀸 𒊺 𒌷 ˄ 𒄀

The planners in the metropolis ordered the well drilled too close to the village cemetery. one must not drink the water, it is saturated with the souls of their dead.

above the well, the airspace has become so rank with gently malign melancholy that commercial flights must be rerouted.

UNE LANGUE, C'EST UN DIALECTE QUI POSSÈDE DE
une langue, c'est un dialecte qui possède de

UNE ARMEE, UNE MARINE ET UNE AVIATION.
IF A LANGUAGE IS A DIALECT WITH AN ARMY
une armee, une marine et une aviation.
if a language is a dialect with an army

AND A NAVY, THEN DICTIONARIES ARE BOTH
and a navy, then dictionaries are both

ITS *EINSATZGRUPPEN* AND ITS *AKRITOI*
its *einsatzgruppen* and its *akritoi*.

....BUT IN LIEU OF AN ARMY AND A NAVY, A STOCK EXCHANGE WILL DO.....

AN EMPIRE THREE
CENTURIES PAST ITS
PRIME IS A JOKE.

AN EMPIRE THREE
DECADES PAST ITS
PRIME IS A KILLING
JOKE.

THE STATE
IS NEITHER
SOVEREIGN NOR
CRISIS MANAGER
NOR ENFORCER
OF THE SOCIAL
CONTRACT.
THE STATE IS A
MAGICIAN – FOR
IT MAKES PEOPLE
DISAPPEAR.

BEING SCIONS OF OVER-DEVELOPED SOCIETIES,

HË PËRITËÑTLÝ RËFËRRËD TØ BËÏÑG 'PØ$T©ÏVÏLÏZËD,'

WHEREAS SHE FOUND 'NEOBARBARISM' MORE TO HER LIKING.

The freeway interchanges are named for the dead, and the cemeteries for the titillation of tourists.

UNDEMOLISHED AND LEFT TO THEIR OWN DEVICES. THE DROWNED BRIDGES AND CEMENT APARTMENT BLOCKS TOOK ON NEW LIFE AS HAZARDS TO NAVIGATION.

To facilitate both tracking and enumeration, all endangered fauna have been issued passports and the various heights of forest canopy have been rigorously standardized.

HOLDING TO MODERN TENETS OF APPROPRIATE TECHNOLOGY, MASS-PRODUCTION COMMENCED NOT WITH HIGH-OCCUPANCY GAS CHAMBERS, BUT WITH HOES APPLIED FORCEFULLY TO THE BACKS OF SKULLS ๑ะ

WENT TO THE WORLD BANK TO WITHDRAW THE WORLD, CUZ I WAS TIRED OF TRYING TO SAVE IT.

BUT THERE WAS A WITHDRAWAL LIMIT OF 3 COUNTRIES PER DAY.

SO I TOOK OUT KIRGHIZIA, KAZAKHSTAN AND SOUTH KOREA, (My favorite bits of Asia).

TOMORROW, I'M GOING BACK FOR THE NORTH AMERICAN FREE TRADE AREA.

Which was it again

The sleep of reason

THAT BREEDS MONSTERS,

OR ITS DREAM?

although illiterate, the uniformed machinegun-toting 13 year old reads his orders perfectly:

FREE WORLD.

FREE MARKET.

TAKE ONE.

Metropolographical Expeditionary Report No. 47

THE EMPEROR'S DIRTY LAUNDRY,

OR

A Tale of Seven Cities Remade to Measure.

SUMMARY

Something is stalking the Great Cities of the World. Something unseemly and insidious. Throttling neighborhood streets with young coxcombs and popinjays sporting skinny-legged jeans. Cratering cozily familiar landscapes with shrapnel by Koziol, Alessi, and Philippe S+arck. Shivving well-tempered skylines with gigantic (and incontinent) edifices resembling nothing so much as ruptured brass artichokes and crumpled tin cauliflowers. A Great Game is afoot, and expeditioning by intermunicipal subterranean railways, by occasional sundry other conveyances, as well as deep within the bowels of innumerable boutique cafés, this excursionist will not rest until he has arrived at the very source of that Greatness itself.

KEY WORDS
agave, coelacanth, gunship, imperial, metropolitan, reposeur, samovar

The Storied Ur-Conurbation of Gan 'Edhen.

I ask you, gentle reader, to reflect upon what is fast becoming of our metropoles. There was a time when a Great City of the World could be known by the stout forms of three constituents—the counting house, the government house, and the opera house—venerated institutions, each an anchor for the civil deportment of a genteel citizenry. But now we see such touchstones collapsing all about us, replaced by a seemingly omnipresent irruption of tumescent edifices whose very forms dissemble hidden functions in our midsts. Attendant upon these we likewise see the appearance of a new caste of gentry, marked by a shambolic aspect inexplicably at odds with their demonstrated efficacy in wittily embellishing streetfronts and shop offerings, amending land rents and cafés per capita, and through their very presence conferring Greatness upon a city of the world. Inquiries into this efficacy will elicit naught but ironic smirks, as though the mere asking proves the questioner's risible obsolescence.

But inquire we must.

Our cities now rise and fall in the shadow of luxuriantly grotesque and enigmatic edifices, their denizens a cryptic cabal of ostentatiously dressed-down dandies. There is taint of subtle sedition here, of secret societies and alien influence, of illicit trafficking in the very stuff of Greatness. Clearly a Great Game is afoot, and thus I have resolved to mount an expedition the purpose of which is to locate the source of that Greatness itself. The expedition, for evident reasons, takes as its object those metropoles most newly ascendant by reason of being most sorely besieged. Indeed, until quite recently their very existences were mere rumors, places lost to legend, expunged from any reputable map. But the expansion of airship service, and of the intermunicipal subterranean railways - 'the Intertubes' in vulgar parlance—has vouchsafed revelation, and so I sally forth to my first terminus: the city of Cibola.

I sit ensconced in a café, its S+arck designed interior surfaces and fittings filigreed with understated Churrigueresque. At my elbow crouches a Koziol bowl of xocolatl frappe, poised atop caricatured silver clawfeet. That is my métier, to *repousez-vous autour* or, perhaps more aptly, *resposez-vous auteur*. I am a credentialed reposeur, sitting ensconced in cafés while texting about what comes within range of sight. It is a job in high demand. In fact, merely advising distant entrepôts on how to attract my sort has become a vocation in itself. It is writ of safe passage to a well-traveled and lavishly-catered life for cadres of self-anointed urban alchemists boasting recipes for transmuting any terra incognita into a Great City of the World. And so I am imported from place to place, myself and my thumb-scrivenings part of the regalia that effects the transmutation and simultaneously proves it has already

The Former Site of the Temple of State of Cibola.

occurred. Would any Great City, after all, be great to begin with were we not spreading word of its Greatness or, more deliciously, any laughable lack thereof, far and wide?

What does not come into sight, however, is no less important than what does. The plaza just beyond the café patio—the ceremonial heart of this city of Cibola back when it was the center of a world—was, not long ago, ringed with buildings of uncertain disposition, half completed or perhaps half demolished, rebar jutting from spiraled columns at the top floors. Drifting amidst them one would have found adolescents garbed in frayed hand-me-downs and respirators filled with cobbler's glue, and aging caballeros in black leather chaps and little else. All gone now, likely sent to be rendered into saleable organs and lubricant for industrial machinery. Instead you will find, as in most any city nowadays from Agartha to Asgard, prefabricated lofts concealed behind impeccable new façades. Although here in Cibola, the façades are newly built with subtle evocations of the ornately antique Plateresque style. Their forecourts bustle with fastidiously bed-headed and unshaven dandies, stuffed into reproduction vintage jeans and diaphanously thinned t-shirts bearing artfully faded prints, and a light dusting of tribal people brought in from the countryside for provision of authentic local color.

Across this scene wanders an elderly man, small and slight. He moves from table to table with a modish Alessi whisk playfully formed to resemble a comical waterboarded stickman. His job is to froth patrons' bowls of premium hot xocolatl when they have gone flat. In exchange he gathers small gratuities. I, however, pay him considerably more, an invitation to serve unwittingly as native guide by regaling me with the history of this place. It is, after all, the regrettable but necessary circumstance of my work that with so much transit from place to place, one seldom has the luxury of knowing much about anyplace oneself.

Long gone, he tells me, are the days when you could know a man's place by the abundance and opulence of his piercings. Back then, one could intuit all one wished from the elongation of an earlobe or the dimension of a labret. The young, in turn, found great pleasure and popularity in finding new and unexpected places to pierce, using materials pointedly selected to strike their elders and betters as common or even unsanitary.

Then the galleons appeared. Their glazed steel bulks devoured the sky as they came ashore to make their way overland with surprising speed, laying dense webworks of the intertubes' pipeline before and behind as they went. But what these sky-scraping factory ships did to space was nothing compared to what they did to time. Silently, they processed it into finer and finer slices and points that found their way into every crevice, crack, pore and alveolus. Surgical masks proved no help, no matter how ingeniously decorated with eagle beaks, jaguar snouts, skeletal mandibles, &c., although the decorating and wearing of masks did provide marks of rank and considerable amusement.[1] When the epidemic reached its height, multitudes found themselves lethally afflicted with being too late, entirely out of date or, most deadly of all, just plain backwards.

As the plague subsided, survivors arose to find their world and its wealth—animal, vegetable, mineral, ancestral, deifical and digital—dissected, dismantled, and sucked down the tubes, only to reemerge from the invader's distant workshops as taxidermied divinities, platinum plated bejeweled memento mori or recipes for stuffed gold leaves. The galleons had anchored themselves at the city's heart and ground its monuments, including the personage of the city's Great Speaker himself, to foundational rubble beneath them. Causeways arching gracefully over floating gardens had become expressways bypassing landfill. And where the Temple of State had loomed now squatted an immense edifice that looked like nothing so much as a mangled titanium agave, packed with such few choice fragments of the city's sights, sounds and affects as evaded pilferage. Many of these fragments in turn decayed beyond recognition as the edifice proved irremediably incontinent, and were replaced in the exhibition halls and adjacent giftshop by copies cast in cleverly inappropriate materials to quote ironically the originals.

Displaced and disoriented in their own grand boulevards, the Great City of their

---

1. *The skeleton remains to the present a source of ambivalent amusement for the locals, commonly depicted in advertising and on protective amulets as riding a combine harvester while glowering anxiously at his pocketwatch.*

The Devouring of the Sky.

World now subject to a world of Great Cities, Cibola's survivors necessarily undertook extreme measures to adapt. Over the course of subsequent years, decades, indeed centuries up to the present, the Cibolaros took to masking themselves first in the invaders' gilt-embroidered velvets, and later in their pinstriped woolens. And as the invaders seemed particularly convinced of the civilizing influence of hats,[2] survivors took cover beneath bowlers, boaters, Stetsons, fedoras, porkpies, &c., and, ultimately, baseball caps. Not that the invaders much noticed or cared, and as it turned out each innovation to come through the tubes was already old hat back at its source. And so the survivors cast off each outflow of exported surplus for the next, with only the most provincial of tribal people knowing no better than to don a remnant gilt-embroidered velvet ball-cap.

Or so I am told. The tribals in the plaza before me, however, seem to have occupied that vital location knowingly, garbed in velvets of their own devising, heavily embroidered upon with ever more ingeniously tangled pinstripes, motifs giving the appearance of nothing so much as spiderwebs rent and ruptured from within. These they wear with pointed assertion, complemented by baseball caps (in colors specific to their moieties) so undersized as to suggest parody and, perhaps as ancestral homage, by surgical masks ornamented with derisively caricatured likenesses of the invaders themselves. Peering more

2. Long years later and half a world away, the city of Janaidar's ruling junta endeavored to ward off a similar threat of invasion with a diktat proclaiming that "now more than ever it is essential to go on wearing hats."

A Distant Giftshop's Showcase of Taxidermied Deities.

intently across the vast square, it becomes clearer that these tribals are not just sitting in the forecourts. Rather, they are embroidering, aggressively. Almost as though they are embroidering at passersby. And then I begin to discern that some of them are not tribals at all. Rather, their number includes young scions of the city, similarly dressed and masked, and militantly wielding embroidery needles themselves.

I depart directionless, accompanied only by the eldster's tale, redacted as an affordable pocket-sized codex conveniently proffered by the teller himself, but upon exiting delicately appropriate the xocolatl whisk as well. There is something ominously amiss about it that belies its gelastic countenance. And its provenance, advertised prominently on the café shop shelves, was the marketplaces of Medina al-Nuhhas.

To say my work consists of sitting in cafés is a disparaging exaggeration. It also entails sitting in tube station waiting lounges, and in the passenger compartments of subterranean carriages. Take the tubes intercity with sufficient frequency, all the lounges and compartments alloy into a single sleek betwixting of pale translucent skins undulating across osseous struts, trusses, pillars, and giftshops, a bardo suspended outside time and space. Aerial travel may well be more romantic, and there

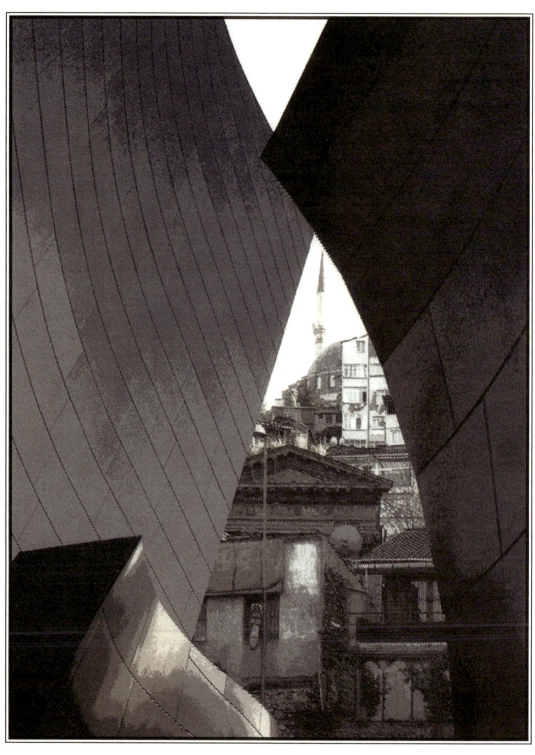

Al-Nuhhas through Its Preemptively Abandoned Reliquary.

remain those affluent few for whom such romance is irresistible. How else would Virgin Tropospheric maintain its airships aloft? But does anybody truly believe their advertisements, touting the superior practicality of reaching any place, anyplace at all, upon the surface of the earth? If a place is not embraced within the tubes' web, after all, can that place truly be said to exist? There is nothing outside the web. Or, at least, certainly not for long.

I perch atop a jewel-toned vase-shaped stool that is suspiciously not quite exactly like those by S+arck for Kartell, in a teahouse of great antiquity, or so the refined minimalism of the interior design coyly suggests—incised and scraped away at strategic points to reveal faded arabesques layered over byzantine mosaic fragments. The tiny, Steuben-esque teaglass in front of me is complemented by a Damien Hirst inspired hubble-bubble in the form of a lung encrusted with black Swarovskoid crystals. Both the chai and the smoke are oversweetly redolent with the flavor of açaí, I find myself missing the distant days of some few months past when pomegranate's sourness was the flavor of choice.

The tearoom is open to a narrow canyon of a street between high apartment walls, choked with similar low stools and tables to turn the entire thoroughfare into a single distended open air café. The walls of Medina al-Nuhhas (or simply al-Nuhhas to the locals), the City of Brass, frame

panoramic slices of city—a mountainous heap of innumerable styles deposited in built strata one atop the other over centuries, all studded with transmission towers that, at regular intervals throughout the day, blanket the city with the sanctified cacophony of simulcast supplications to the divine.

The canyon walls are punctuated with uncountable oriels, covered balconies, and soffits jutting wildly from rooftop terraces. Not long ago one would have seen matriarchs leaning over these, careful not to catch on the splintered gingerbread carvings of the splintering wooden edges, lowering buckets on strings to merchants below. And there were always merchants below, the vegetable and gas and battery mongers giving way as day wore into evening to song mongers and transvestite sex mongers and ecstatically dancing enlightenment mongers in towering headgear.

But now the cobalt lenses of apotropaic eyes, electronically conjoined to hidden and heavily armed sentinels, glare warily at all such vagabonds. The bay windows and balconies are sealed, scaffolded and safety-netted as their ornamental railings and reliefs are painstakingly restored to original condition and, as at Belovodye and Kêr-Is and any other aspirant Great City of the World, their interiors are transformed into condominiums and serviced holiday rentals. Underneath, fauxhawked popinjays sprawl across every low table, poured into antiquely-styled jeans and prefabricatedly worn t-shirts topped with trucker's caps, pecking at keypads of diverse sorts. Those, and a few remaining matriarchs thoughtfully fingering their iBeads, one of whom has clearly noted I am not local. Sitting down on the stool beside me she orders our teaglasses refilled, makes introduction, and tells me of what she rightly suspects my cursory views can not reveal.

Long gone, she tells me, are the days when you could know a man's place by the shape and size of his hat. There were hats for every occasion and every social faction, with especially elaborate ones awarded as honorifics. Whether conversing beneath the deeply eaved pavilions of the public fountains or cruising through the straits, a true gentleman displayed his headwear proudly and, upon death, even preferred to be buried under a stone replica of the hat he had worn in life. Insofar as a covered head is a mark of civilization, this was the Great City of the World when other such cities had been little more than bare-headed villages. Not to be in and of the city was to be hopelessly jejune; anybody wishing to be somebody took up residence behind the bay windows of the city's timbered escarpments. They came from everywhere and were welcomed, even minorities enjoyed no small degree of suffrage provided they were willing to pay the nominal surcharge and refrain from wearing slippers in colors proscribed their class.

Then, the disbelievers arrived. At first their ambassadors, distinct in the dark velvets of their gilt-embroidered t-shirts and matching ballcaps, were given polite audience in the outermost court of the Federal Palace and then sent on their ways. But in time, embassies followed upon the ambassadors' footsteps, and wedged themselves into al-Nuhhas' summits. Some were built like many-layered glass houses, easy to see out of but as difficult to look into as a hall of mirrors. Others were built like classically columned and pedimented bunkers, windowless Vitruvianized concrete spiked all about with closed circuit observation cameras. And from their embassies the ambassadors watched, scrutinizing the city and its people for any hint of being too late, entirely out of date, or just plain backwards. Meanwhile, there were ever more frequent rumors of steel and glass pinnacles sighted sliding through the straits by day, and of gunships lofting silently overhead by night.

Something had to be done. The disbelievers' eyes would have to be persuaded of, and perhaps even slightly unnerved by,

An Exorbitant Architectonic Novelty.

the thoroughly modern civility of the surveilled. And with galleons lurking, perhaps, just offshore, who was to say a little catching up would be such a bad thing? So from the city's heights, the most tastefully sophisticated of makeovers was proclaimed. Dress caftans were remade of velvet and embroidered in gilt, then later remade again in gray wool. The hats of all sizes and shapes that had distinguished one urbanite from the next were banned, and by proclamation the people were united in the wearing of brimmed caps—albeit back to front with the brim to the rear, so as to not interfere with liturgical prostrations.

Once bodies had been so restyled, the spaces of their habitation simply had to follow suit. Divans and poufs were reinterpreted in an international modern style, if not supplanted entirely by the most austere of functionalist furnishings. Mosaic tiled floors were relaid with the most cutting edge linoleum prints. Eventually, entire landmarks were either redecorated from the inside out or abandoned for the construction of less dated edifices. The al-Nuhhasi Shadow of the Divine himself, shortly before his admittedly reluctant conversion to the far less passé title of President,[3] had an entire new palace built in the deconstructionist idiom. Even today the willfully fractured geometries of its grand archways perfectly complement the crumpled tulip form of the immense, stainless steel structure adjacent that would

3. *A gracious sovereign even in his delimited condition, he himself commemorated my arrival by presenting me his own Zippo lighter, bearing his personal calligraphic sigil, and for a most reasonable price following only the most decorous of haggling.*

The Enclosures of Shangri-La, Ante- and Post-Modern.

have been the palace reliquary, had it not been for the steel's intolerable heat gain in summer and the roof's unanticipated permeability during the rainy season.

The enactment of the makeover proclamation spangled the city's mountainous palimpsest with architectonic novelties. But the fiduciary impacts were more dramatic still, draining the treasury and necessitating external wherewithal if the makeover was to be brought to full fruition. Eventually even the embassies were approached, and proved amenable to supplying the necessary lines of credit or, as in the case of the city's new tube station, to undertaking the construction themselves. And when the treasury was emptied entirely, the ambassadors declared the bankruptcy final and definitive proof of backwardness. Reinforced by galleons just offshore and gunships immediately overhead, they took possession of the city's choicest assets and luxuries in situ, liquidated them, and sent them down the tubes, leaving the remainder to slowly decompose for want of maintenance.

To be endemically confronted, by every moldered wall and teetering archway, with the great fall from worldliness of one's own Great City would seem cause for great discontent. And there are indeed some who continue to insist upon, and lobby for, re-admission. But others have found themselves possessed instead by a resiliently bittersweet love of evanescence, patiently savoring the melancholy of decay and creating anew with its revenants. The matriarch, for instance, recasts it into jewelry. She presents me a ring she has forged herself of scrap metals and embossed, in a pidgin of local and ambassadorial tongues,[4] with a concise paean to the powerfully abiding presence of things long gone. Nor, I realize, are the vintage jeans of these dandified Musc'ad-Dins reproductions at all. Rather, they look to have been carefully excavated, recuperated and reconditioned, just as their trucker's caps have been in many instances padded to achieve prodigious widths and exceptional heights. And the wearers themselves are perhaps not so much pecking at their keypads as they are vibrating or even bouncing, as though ready at any moment to burst into ecstatic dance. Distracted, I neglect to notice my own purloinment of the hubble-bubble I had used, its bottom stamped as made in Shangri-La.

I am prone, it seems, to unfair exaggeration. For instance, it may well be true that given enough time en route all tube stations meld into one. And since their earliest incarnations they have as a species tended towards enduring morphological similarities, glazed skins stretched over sterile tortuous guts. But build it larger, prettier and, most important, more distinctively, and more will come. And so here a new station's trusses are arrayed to resemble a clockwork coral reef, there a verdant oasis in a cyclopean Wardian case, countered by another elsewhere splayed like a mechanical dragon in repose, &c. Akin to those in my own position, the small handful of itinerant station builders live like pashas and are upon occasion even formally awarded the title, commissioned by sovereigns the world around to create grand vestibules that confer upon a city its Greatness at its own doorstep.

4. Only these latter dialects being commonly referred to by the locals as languages, having come well-equipped as they did with armies and navies or, more recently, stock exchanges.

I posture stiffly on a Southern Official's style armchair reinterpreted by S+arck in transparent polycarbonate, and sip a lapsang souchong latte dispensed from a neoprene-wrapped Eva Solo samovar. The gray stone of the surrounding courtyard has been newly repointed and hung all about with olive green curtains, the wooden stairways and upturned cornices

winkingly repainted in contrasting red. The courtyard's ornamented minimalism accentuates a cleverly dispersed mélange of heroically realist chinoiserie collectibles, their eclecticism at odds with the uniformity of the foppish clientele's greased shag-cuts, precisely gauged facial stubble, and obligatory antiqued jeans,[5] relieved only by a smattering of local personages in anticly printed pajamas.

I ask the proprietor, a former state geomancer with a long goatee artfully grayed to suggest venerability, about the provenance of the collectibles, and he tells me they were all possessions of the courtyard's resident family when the space was conveyed to him out from under them. I wince, and he elaborates by way of both illumination and, I suspect, justification.

Long gone are the days when you could barely know a person's place, men and women alike side by side in identical button-front pajamas and caps to match. Not that time and style stood still. Sartorial change accompanied each change of administration—from long sleeves to short, stand collars to fall, more pockets or less, black to gray to blue or back again, a brimmed cap or a beanie. But the changes applied to all, albeit more masterfully tailored in finer materials for officials.

Courtyards, however, were another matter. The vast plateau of the city of Shangri-La, or Kalapa to its natives, was thick with gray stone enclosed courtyards, and courtyards within courtyards. You could know an individual's and family's place alike by the size, condition and furnishing of their courtyard. Great lineages of administrators boasted vast expanses of self-consciously selected and preciously manicured heirloom ornamentals, whereas those of lesser descent tended more towards compact arrangements of old rubber tires and corrugated cardboard in desperate want of recycling. And a neighborhood's place could be known alike. Each district of the city was, as it still is, favored with its own garden park—a courtyard for the masses complete with miniature menageries inhabiting miniature palaces sited amongst miniature seas, miniature mountains, and miniature golf courses (the last most often to be found, by dint of self-evident geomantic rationale, in near adjacency to the requisite animal sacrifice pavilion). They were a delight to all, their general confinement to official use notwithstanding.

Until the ghosts[6] came. Their galleons scraped deep scars across heaven as they anchored on the coast, and traded voraciously for teas, motherboards, high-performance athletic footwear, silk, &c. But the ghosts had little of interest to exchange in return, other than their own promissory notes. In time, of course, those notes had to be paid, and when that time arrived they insisted on making repayment in nicotine, caffeine, high fructose corn syrup, &c. Addiction, after all, being a great guarantor of market stability. These terms of payment having been refused, the ghosts responded by delivering lessons in

---

5. The frequency of such Jack-a-dandies' co-incidence with spaces of titivation has come to strike me as uncanny, and it is my conviction that subsequent inquiry into possible directions of causality will, if sufficiently resourced, prove most fruitful.

6. The correct rendering of this term from the local tongue as "westerly ocean's and airways' alien ghost devil folk", while more thorough, loses a certain concision in translation.

Ghostly Instruction Delivered in a Garden Park Pavilion.

The Styling of a City for the World.

7. This perhaps having served as originary inspiration for the oft-quoted local proverb "modernity grows out of the barrel of a Gatling gun". Also, see appended plates I and II.

civility that took the much commemorated form of gunships thoroughly incinerating the city's garden parks from overhead,[7] although not without exhibiting the common decency to first perfunctorily loot their contents.

Subsequently imported cases of soft drinks and cartons of cigarettes notwithstanding, the ghosts met only inconstant success in expanding their anchorage more than briefly, and in time retreated back offshore or even withdrew their flotillas entirely. In tandem the city experienced paroxysms, waxings and wanings, but prospered more often than not, and eventually the officials decided Shangri-La was fit to assume on its own terms its place as a Great City of the World, neither belated nor out of date nor, most importantly, backwards at all. And so they set to the acquisition of everything necessary to style the city for the world, and its citizens as worldly. In this the ghosts were exceedingly useful, given both that they already had Great Cities of the World, and not incidentally a great deal of outstanding indebtedness to repay for it.

The ghosts' most gifted master builders were imported en masse, bearing schemes from home enlarged and elaborated into the most experimentally grandiose of tessellated, disequilibriated, even impossibly curvaceous of edifices. Along with a design for an opulently serpentine tube station,

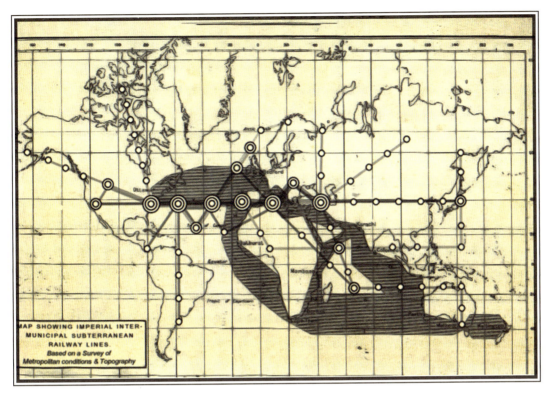

A Scratch-Cradle of Meridians.

of course. Improbable as they were, work commenced on all, excepting one scheme for a Palace of Culture in the gigantic form of a mutilated anodized aluminum lotus, still under study for its seemingly evident unsuitedness to inclement weather.

To build, however, there must be space, a conspicuous absence amidst the labyrinth of courtyards nested so densely each within and beside the next. So by official mandate vast swathes of the city were reduced to rubble and the rubble leveled flat, and residents exiled by official pronouncement to identically featureless concrete tenements newly built just beyond and beneath the pale of urbanization. Not that the city entire was demolished. Many courtyards were adopted by the presiding officials themselves, and sensitively restored to pristine condition for the appreciation of sufficiently cultured persons.

To build, there must also be muscle, all the more when there is so much to build. And to this end, a system of corvée was discretely instituted. By official decree young able-bodied peasants were compelled to build Shangri-La's Greatness, first driven into the city and Impressed into construction gangs, then driven back out again once the job was done. A Great City of the World, after all, is no place for backwards and benighted peasant conscripts.

With all the monumental artifacts of au courant urbanity now irrupting from

Memorials to the Anticipated Triumphs of the "Let's Forward" Decree.

out the gray stone matrix of the city's vast plateau, officials have begun settling into their commandeered courtyards to savor their hard earned leisure. A growing number are even having their regulation pajamas retailored in pinstriped gray, and going entirely bareheaded. But it seems, as I survey the courtyard all about me, they look with mounting unease at the more colorfully clad enfants terrible in their midst, taking pajamas printed with polychromatic "Louie Vitton" monograms and "Nkie" swooshes for excessively outré, uncultured, perhaps even insinuating solidarity with the Nkie and Rebok clad corvée laborers just beyond the walls. Which, the proprietor whispers, is precisely what they are intended to insinuate. Perhaps this is why closed circuit surveillance cameras surmount the courtyard wall, directed both outside and in. By all indications, the officials must be very afraid.

Be that as it may, I despair aloud at setting my next course by such querulous gallants, let alone pocket codices or xocolatl whisks or rhinestone-encrusted hubble-bubbles. To which the former geomancer cocks an eyebrow and replies, obliquely, "Ah yes, all made here, export quality. For Avalon."

It is said[8] that a Great City of the World in want of a grand tube station shall likewise

8. In the broadsheets of the Rockmen's and Excavators' guild, most prominently.

want for Greatness and the world. The inverse of this, however, I have found to be entirely another matter. Many are now the times I have, in transferring from one carriage to another, briefly exited the hygienically uniform bowels of the tubes in search of sun and wind, neither artificial nor recirculated, only to step out into frigid tundra or foetid swamp. Such is the happenstance leaving of our passage, a scratch-cradle of meridians drawn between terminal destinations, indifferent to the terrain of their own mutual crossing. And for every crossing a station, each a shining opportunity for local chieftains and warlords to amend their tent-strewn steppe or bungalow-choked mangrove with causeways, conning towers, mooring masts, duty-free malls, &c. Cast abruptly skywards to loom over stoop-shouldered yurts or spindly-legged stilt huts, such vast agglomerations of glazed steel tracery yield cities where there are none, so as to make a name for themselves and scatter it amongst those abroad upon the face of the whole earth.

I squat upon a patchwork mat, before me a plank set atop a balding tire. From off this I sip murky tea directly out of a screw-topped half-liter bottle, and gaze across a no less murky river. A dive, it would appear on casual glance, cobbled together from dispossession, divestment, and wartime stringency. But in fact, the mat is tiled of silk brocades painstakingly gleaned by FLOR from the estates of this city's most dissolutely spendthrift suzerains, the plank Bang & Olufsen's graft of data ports and infrared links to endangered old-growth teak, the tire a rim of black sheet steel delicately laser-etched by Studio Tord Boontje with belts of entwined naga silhouettes plying transoceanic shipping routes. The archly subversive bottle is glass handblown in Chihuly's own studio, and the reedy murk within only the uppermost of first bud leaves hand-picked by the most meticulously trained of imported lemurs, blended with the finest kelps harvested by the agile tentacles of no less thoroughbred octopuses. Only the nostalgia for a simpler age of threadbare necessity is what it appears, but pendant upon imaginings of those too young to have themselves survived from off of newly minted ruins.

The river too is artifice, continuously regurgitated to meander between brocaded silken banks, as might be expected in a delicately rusticated transit salon newly suspended by S+arck amidst the airship anchorages high atop the tube termini of the city's central station. And as might be expected from so lofty a perch, the ingenuity of this bardo's furnishings is inevitably eclipsed by the vistas beyond. Assiduously ill-groomed maccaronis, an aerostocracy garbed in deliberately retrograde touring accoutrements, jockey for tables nearest the perversely miniscule opalescent portholes.[9] Over objections, I have preempted one such table for myself—those with my credentials are, after all, uniquely qualified to divine from so elevated a perspective all that is worth

9. *Picture windows being confined exclusively to the floors of the open-plan lavatories, providing both spectacular views and expedient drainage directly to the streets far below.*

His Exaltedness' Flagship.

knowing of a place. The city of Traitrueng obligingly unscrolls its palimpsest beneath me, but vexes with its cacographics. Leaved thickly one atop another, shreds of steepled shrine and castle keep relict marginalia in a dense collage of godowns, punctuated and struck through with high glazed turrets, swathed in a mucilage of corrugated fiberglass market stalls and bound with the illuminated knotwork of expressways writ over long-desiccated rivers. Although merely passing through en route to Avalon, I come nonetheless prepared, in this instance with the guidebook authorized by the local Ministry of Savage Enlightenment—a garbled translation of the institution's true name no doubt, given the logical absurdity of enlightening anything savagely—and thoughtfully provided by means of automated periodical dispensers throughout the station.

This is not the Traitrueng of romantically exoticized imaginings, I read. Long gone, the guide informs me in charmingly fractured language, are the days when you could know a man's place by the elegant complexity of his layered brocades, the circuitously elaborated gentility of his speech, the caliber of his finely damascened sidearms and the number of manufactory-floor villeins who bore his tattoo upon their persons. Within these manufacties the latest varietals of polished grains, of crossbred garlands, of infused whiskies and spiced cigarettes and sundry other household necessities were assembled en masse and ensouled by the city's shamans. Traitrueng's castes of significance were thus ensured sufficient nourishment, entertainment, and social advantage to require little congress beyond the city's gates, necessitating that imported diplomats and the occasional misrouted outsider[10] cluster at river's edge, keypads in hand, to pilfer bandwidth from metropolitan Bhogavati on the opposite bank (much as Bhogavati augmented its own Greatness through periodic pilferage of Traitrueng's citizenry, counting houses, and athletic associations; and Janaidar of Bhogavati's; &c.). And such clockwork playthings as might still be lacking could be had from the sole galleon suffered upon occasion to anchor on Traitrueng's furthest edge.

So the coming of outsiders was unremarkable. The sudden arrival of an armada of them, however, overshadowed by a swarm of gunships escorts and demanding immediate and indefinite moorage, was another matter entirely. A matter to which sidearms offered no effective rebuttal regardless how numerous, finely damascened, highly calibered or, in a last desperate effort, shamanically ensouled. A matter that refused resolution even when Traitrueng's creative castes, as show of hospitality no less than for the novelty, augmented their brocades with evocations of the outsiders' somber velvets (albeit embroidered with motifs of gilded tentacles interwoven atop naga scales) and took to growing muttonchops or mighty handlebar moustaches—an admirable accomplishment given the local propensity towards glabrescence.

And so a tenth of the of the city was ceded as harborage to the outsiders, who proceeded to pilot their galleons on a roundabout course that effectively sequestered a quarter of the city while leaving half again as much scoured bare in the vessels' wakes. And worse, they still had not even dropped anchor.

The city's Exalted Gatekeeper himself, long thought a puppet of neighborhood leigelords and their generals,[11] seized the initiative with issuance of the "Let's Forward" decrees, proscribing anything too late, out of date, or just plain backwards and mandating progress for all excepting, of course, the leatherworkers, mutagenic waste handlers, and similarly untouchable castes. Suzerains and villeins alike were enlisted for the city's immediate intubation, then intrepid explorers camouflaged in the best pinstriped woolens and sent down those tubes to discover just which direction 'forward' might be. Streets and alleys were first festooned with talking wires, then spiked instead with cellular relay towers pleasingly concealed as pipal trees. Manufactures worked through the nights as expeditions' specimens (and even personal souvenirs) refluxed out the tubes to be improved upon, reproduced, and promptly ensouled, thus giving birth to roving troupes of solid-state gramophones, digital kinetoscopes, microwave heliographs, &c. These in turn found

10. The more previously commonplace term, outrageous big-nosed redheads, now being regarded as sorely impolitic.

11. Literally an ensouled poppet, as rumor has it, although the guide assures he is a most hospitable one pleased to host flawless automated demonstrations of ritual song and dance dedicated to the spirits of ancestral engineers and ergonomists, and at no charge to wayfarers. This I found to be accurate in the breach, as His Exaltedness' shamans compel upon departure the purchase of extravagant battery-operated talismans against obsolescence, travel interruptions, low rates of investment return, &c. To date, however, my talismans have worked faultlessly.

shelter in the ephemerally béton brutalist warehouses and makeshift market halls that germinated in the voided wakes of passing galleons. Traitrueng overtopped the very now, the entirely of-the-moment and the fully forwards by days, weeks, even months, raising commemorative monuments in indigenized muscular Gothic to its impending successes and rendering its own creations obsolete at the moment of their production. Yet none of it abated the outsiders' demands, if anything they had become measure-for-measure more insistent, and still their galleons gouged deep furrows through the city.

In the midst of these events arrived a report from an explorer dispatched to the outsiders' very hearth, making plain at last which way was forward. To wit:

> "Long gone are the days before the outsiders raised themselves from nothing to sup upon stuffed gold leaves while they platinize the dead. Or so they would believe. Yet here the evidence is all about that their xocolatl, their samovars, their very Greatness is not of their own devising but has been gathered only lately, and that from distant shores. Why mightn't others do as well?"

Production commenced immediately on His Exaltedness' own galleons and gunships, wrought in the chicest idioms of structural expressionism and blobisimus respectively, each further ahead of its time than the last and all thoroughly invested with only the most indignant of souls. Why should Traitrueng want for taxidermied deities, bejeweled hubble-bubbles, lapsang souchong lattes? The outsiders would be driven from a Traitrueng made great again, great enough to liberate poor backwards Bhogavati as well, then Shangri-La, then Janaidar, and farther horizons still, even should they need be—with only the greatest of regret, of course—razed in the doing. And so, let's forward!

The guidebook concludes on this clarion's call, leading the reader to postulate the final victory. And inarguably Traitrueng has prospered. But a downward glance reveals fresh bare gashes dredged across the city, and newish tenements that erupt from out what appear as nothing so much as lately blasted craters. Nor, dropping another coin into the thermal-imaging spyglass mounted to the saloon wall, can I miss the shambling indigenous galleon boilers and limping airship engines. They march obstructively along the expressway amidst ragged phalanxes of abandoned household commodities, servomotors grinding angrily, in protest against their premature obsolescence. Backpack-beladen maccaronis watch the event enraptured, indeed such processions are sold to them as preeminent sights of interest. But the locals, evident at this distance by the logos of their employers embroidered prominently in gold across their pinstriped sack suits, avert their gazes compunctiously and move on.

I could text of many more cities. I am, after all, given writ of passage to one after

The Mystery before the Viceroyalty.

A Mystery, Solved.

the other and a generous stipend on the promise I will do precisely that. They believe their fortunes depend, at least in part, upon my doing so. Cities where you could once have known a man's place by the fullness of his beard, or by the print on his skirt, or by the number of husbands his wife had acquired. There is, however, space for only so many ciphers in one text, and only so many cities that have recompensed me adequately to warrant my full promotional mention. And besides, my thumbs grow weary. So I will conclude instead from a mother city, a mother of cities, a place to which all tubes must lead—great Avalon herself.

I sprawl across a seat that, beneath its cigarette burns, missing leg, and impastos of duct tape, must once have been S+arck's plasticized reimagining of an overstuffed club chair. Within arm's reach, dense veils of acrid smoke disgorge from the exhaust stacks of a continuous procession of motorcarriages. I squint through the miasma and over the lip of a beaker filled with pre-soddened tea leaves, warily served me by a Cibolaro expatriate, that in bone china would make for a delicately subversive recasting of a crumpled disposable plastic cup. Except that it is, in fact, merely plastic, creased by repeated use. Arrayed in single file along the meager sidewalk is a motley assortment of similarly distressed furniture occupied, as in any City of the World, by shambolic young fribbles intent to the exclusion of all else upon their keypads. But unlike elsewhere, they display a refreshing if perhaps unintended honesty—their jeans and t-shirts faded, frayed and peeled with mere neglect, their hair lank and faces stubbled from simple inattention.

There may have been a time when things were otherwise, but I am at a loss to know. Those about me admit no recognition of any past, nor for the most part of strangers in general, responding to inquiries with silent disacknowledgement or, at most, a glare of withering disapproval. Which is not to imply an utter dearth of intercourse, as with repeated queries into the provenance of my al-Nuhhasi ring; my Belovodyite aeronaut's pocket chronograph; even the pince nez I acquired shortly after my arrival here in Avlun, its narrowly slit lenses relieving the city's drab grey skies and indistinguishably grey skyline with the semblance of a simulated horizon. My responses, however, consistently incite from the Avlunians what seem looks of jealously resentful hunger.

This is not what I had expected from Avalon, that mother of cities, but then again this is not the Avalon I had expected. It is, in fact and quite literally, a different one. Avalon the mater polis had many provinces, built in each an Avalon of its own, and it is to one of these—Avlun to its locals—I erroneously booked passage. I would have rerouted on the spot, were it not for the fact (as the borderguards irritably informed me) that Avlun takes a dim view of illicit emigration. My departure would require a writ of exit, the provision of which was beyond their authority. To which was added, with utmost conspicuousness, disdain for any who would wish to leave so Great a City of the World.

Attempts to locate where writs of exit might be obtained have proven fruitless, as for instance along the sidewalk café where my inquiries briefly break the tatterdemalion jackanapes from their sullen caffeinated silences into brusque insistences, verging upon hysteria. Avlun the loyal, doting scion of Avalon's shining shores; Avlun the tolerant, safe haven for the exiles of the world; Avlun the egalitarian, its hospices open to even the lowliest of laborers come their appointed hour; Avlun, Great City of the World! Would I prefer to be amongst the pestilential hordes of Shangri-La, knee-deep in the gore of insurrection that fills Cibola's streets, drowned within poor inundated Atlantis' deluged halls? Would I prefer to be too late, entirely out of date, or just plain backwards?

These intonations seem surpassing strange. In part, try as I may I recollect no plague in Shangri-La, nor blood-bathed revolution in Cibola. But that aside, even the most perfunctory glance along this very street reveals a tide of bagged refuse rising against the most generic of boxy cement buildings—a precious few having at most addenda like crystal keloids or biopsied tin tumors of dubious climatic suitability belatedly affixed with grudging expediency to update their façades—all plastered thickly with wheatpasted broadsheets. The entire fluoresces luridly in the glare of outsize praxinoscopes projecting slogans urging resolute commitment to drudgery, propriety in deportment, and the maintenance of 'mental hygiene', interspersed with rudely animated advertisements for expired commodities 'coming soon'. I bemusedly remark aloud upon the oxymorons of desultory and emulated Greatness, only to elicit those disapproving glares, followed by resounding silences that abruptly deny my very presence.

Uncertain of where next to proceed I stand immobilized at kerbside, attracting the attention of a passing hackney carriage. The hackman, a tawny Quiviran, asks after my destination and, slyly, I respond merely that I must go secure a writ. He motions me inside and we are off, the hackman discoursing all the while (as is the wont of those who ply his trade) upon the passing scenery. A dank and weedchoked park incites the tale of Avlun's inauspicious foundation upon an implacably sucking mire. A moldering triumphal arch collapsed across a derelict airship hangar yields the story of how distant Avalon forsook this backwater to its own devices. A team of Atlanteans picking through refuse bags evokes a lengthy explication of how the wendigo[12] now subsist from off such flotsam, jetsam, and castaways as wash up from off of passing galleons or (and here he winks mischievously at me) stumble misrouted and lost from out the tubes. And arriving at what the hackman announces as the Palace of the Viceroyalty, he chuckles at the monumental statue on front, mysteriously headless. Ironically appropriate, he asserts, as no king in living memory has noticed to appoint a viceroy here.

---

12. The Quiviran term for settlers, of derivation unknown to me.

My meeting with the factotum to the aide-de-camp to the undersecretary to the Avlunian viceroy is brief, after so lengthy a pursuit. Costumed like a mothballed Avalonian diplomat—all faded indigo velvet and peeling gold appliqués - she proclaims Avlun's affluence, hospitality, heroic egalitarianism, &c., remonstrates my desire to depart, and advises with the faintest hint of menace that her government believes one such as myself would do well to instead remain and thumb-scriven of the city's Greatness for all the world to read. I wryly suggest my audience will certainly be most favorably impressed should I report on a detritivorous city slowly sinking into its own paludal miasma, and would no doubt book passage without delay. She fixes me with the glare of disapproval, contemptuously stamps a writ of exit and, before ignoring my presence entirely, summons a Janaidari crusher to see me roughly out the door.

The hackman has awaited me, to continue with his tour. A distant, concrete phalanx of crumbling dormitory towers elicits the history of how the first Atlantean refugees to drift ashore were barracked in those frigid exurban barrens and compelled, as they still are, to work the refuse harvests. And in the neighboring donjon I would find indentured Janaidaris contracted as security guards and, adjacent that, disappeared Cibalero restricted to servitude in bistros. And what of your Quivirans, I ask, to which he answers that his people did not arrive at all. They were here when the wendigo arrived, and would

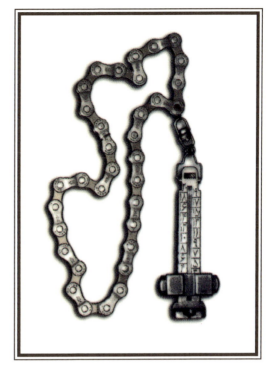

remain once the swamp had finished swallowing them back down again. At which he pilots us around to the palace's backside, and cocks his head at a second monument—the gargantuan bronze of a dignified Avalonian triumphantly holding aloft before him a severed human head graced with distinctly Quiviran features.

Do please forgive the terseness of my tone and the violation of my narrative's symmetry, but present circumstances preclude elegant thumb-scrivening. I find myself wedged tightly between many score of fellow travelers, all of us balanced precariously on crisscrossed tarpaulins and blankets precariously securing mounds of antiquated heliographs, tinned and salted meats and, most vitally, innumerable ladders

A Desert Idyll in the Shadow of the Barzakh.

and knotted climbing ropes and grappling hooks and decrepit oil-stained pneumatic sledge hammers &c. All in turn pile impossibly high atop a motley conveyance assembled of a ramshackle Daimler heavy industries chassis studded with enormous bald tires, tractor treads, sputtering engines and flagging sails. We crawl across a pale scarlet desert accompanied single-file by a baker's dozen of similar conveyances equally overloaded, parallel to a towering agglomeration of thorned hedges, chain-link fences, stone palisades and concrete ramparts festooned with concertina wire and extending viciously beyond the range of sight before and behind. The Barzakh, the drover calls it, his tone a combination of awe and contempt.

This is the storied, endlessly sprawling ur-connurbation of Gan 'Edhen, or Iram of the Pillars Great and Worlded to its locals before they disparagingly rechristened it as Hûrqalyâ. It bears, however, no resemblance to the effulgent depictions on the ancient cartes postales. I would scarce have ventured here myself, were it not for my belated discovery that the Avlunian authorities counterbalanced issuance of my writ of exit with a vindictive failure to return my reposeur's credentials and, thus, my original writ of passage, depositing me sans papiers and baggage here beyond the Barzakh, where the tubes do not deign to reach. I have since acquired a wardrobe comprised of oversized "Hûrqalyâ B" grade hand-me-down garments, their printed CK, D&G and A&F sigils so faded as to be barely discernable, one of the wide-brimmed woven telephony-wire basket hats so favored by the sun-scorched Iramites, and a battered qalamdan of mesmeric ink requisite to forging a new writ of passage. I can only hope that latter will suffice to pass inspection.

Our caravan trudges across endless fields of ruddy salt, strewn about irregularly with toppled stumps and capitals that were once the city's pillars and, occasionally, by the jagged skeletons of derelict galleons assiduously dismantled and scavenged by the Iramites to construct and maintain the very same conveyances upon which we ride. These galleons, the caravan drover relates as he warily coaxes the protesting engines, once carried Iram's bountiful pomegranate harvests far and wide, and bore back Greatness on the return voyage. Then, when the orchards devoured the last of the water and turned the fecund soil to thick slabs of salt stained ruby with residue of grenadine, the galleons enthusiastically carried those off as well, until there was nothing left to bear away at all (de trop kidneys, corneas, partial pancreases, &c. bound for the "crimson market" excepted).

The Barzakh arose soon after, incised across the denuded landscape layer by layer under wary armed guard, its proclaimed intent to interdict the petty smuggling of such reddened salt slabs as remained. "Blood salt", the Great Cities' most greatly worlded luminaries called it with newfound distaste, a rationale scarcely to be believed as no such slabs remained to be smuggled. Now the remnants of Iram traffick exclusively in surplus Cibaleros, Janaidaris,

The Hortus Tyrannicus.

Atlanteans, Bhogavatis, &c., and in me, all seekers of our own imagined Gan 'Edhens.

Our itinerary brooks no deviation. The days are passed in transit beneath the Barzakh's shadow, swaddled and hunched against the perpetual stinging pink dust, music made upon relic keypads and by the oral beating of boxes our sole diversion. But at night we pause furtively, eluding eyes both stationary and airborne, human cargo taking up ladder, rope and hammer to assault the Barzakh under cover of darkness and, perhaps, claw passage through. Some succeed. Others do not. And now, at last, my turn has come. The drover wishes me safe passage, and presses a rosary of upcycled mechanical detritus into my hand. I make selam, hoist a pneumatic hammer, and set to work.

Insofar as the tubes' meridians forge a single city out of many, it is no surprise that there are neighborhoods of bright lights, good repute and better repair, and conversely there are those of lesser reliability that the visitor is best advised not to enter unawares. But to have been deposited beyond the tubes' pale entire and obliged to claw one's way back is another matter entire, one surpassed in its unspeakable indelicacy only by the blunt existence of such a netherworld in the first accounting and, grimmer still, by the dread fact of its unenviable and compulsory inhabitation. All efforts to becalm my sorely frayed composure so as to ponder this revelation in philosophical detachment, however, are sorely frustrated by the overhead ticker display's announcements of repeated boarding deferments, each an insult heaped atop the injury of a journey already so cruelly disrupted. I force my attention instead to the brobdignian televisor in the station's nearest tavern, displaying a sporting match between Atlantis and Shangri-La. Broadcast from Shangri-La's new stadium—a vast nickel-plated carbon fiber phoenix's aerie wedged high between the city's tallest peaks, the Shangri-Lanians play archaically as set forth in their sacred texts. I am told the Atlanteans would win easily, securing a slot against Ker-Is in the semifinals, were it not for their chronic postdiluvian dearth of practice grounds and, exacerbating the matter, what appear to be the initial effects of high altitude oedemata. But in truth I would find the sport of little interest, were it not providing welcome distraction from the nearby ragamuffin clamorously playing at *Grand Theft Vimana: Lankapura Stories*. Indeed, the tavern's offerings may well be all that preclude the necessity of summoning a chirurgeon to extract the gaming engine from the urchin's nether-regions. Even the most freshly abjected fugitive from Hûrqalyâ may be certain that from any bardo there must be, inevitably and ineluctably,[13] rebirth into the world, but it is now apparent there can be no certainty how prompt that rebirth will be.

I sit in a translucent white polycarbonate Louis XVI chair at a translucent white acrylic table in the form of a floating tablecloth, and peruse the voluminous menu at an open-air café subtly themed for the Levantine gauchos of the late Baroque. Hot xocolatl is available, as is scented chai and lapsang souchong lattes alongside matcha smoothies and rooibus creamosas, and sheesha in every flavor available for extraction the world over. For a surcharge, it can be had with a side order of frankincense, or amethyst dust, or platinum shavings. More solid fare is available as well—porcus troianus, kavun dolması, turducken, a comprehensive selection of fine viands doubly and even trebly ensouled by means of the latest technological ingenuities, provided they are stuffed into yet finer fare, and then into finer still. And there is even coelacanth poke or white rhinoceros foie gras to be had as an appetizer, if inquired after with discretion.

Every table is occupied by young coxcombs, fixated upon their sundry keypads, who not long ago would have complemented their carefully neglected coifs with vintage seeming jeans and wryly adopted trucker's caps. And there remain a few of these old skool swells, these incoyables classiques. But even they are now supplementing their wardrobes with opulent

13. *This despite multifarious, and wholly preposterous, legends of travelers condemned, for reason of expired or misvalidated writs, to ride the tubes eternally: cf. "The Rime of the Frequent Flyer" by this author.*

and abundant piercings, ever larger and more elaborate millinery, and pajama tops in black or gray or navy blue. And velvets embroidered with ornate gold pinstriping seem to be making recent inroads amongst the better traveled. Uncertainty as to what may be just ahead of the curve, and what if anything will remain there, commingles with an improvident reluctance to commit to anything at all.

The selfsame profligate confusion teems across the façades adjacent. The walls of Avalon's venerable grand arcade, this fountainhead of civitas, have over time become encrusted with strata of silvered and gilt bas relief, surmounted with carefully verdigris'd copper plates, interrupted by overlapped platinum scales, all wittily gouged by slivers of COR-TEN steel cascading patinas of ochre down frontages studded with a glittering profusion of Swarovski crystals and vigilant electronic eyes. Over and beyond these, visible through the rhodium ribs of the arcade's glazed vault, irrupt the upper reaches of later constructions: an enormous obsidian tesseract, pierced by minute pearlescent portholes; a colossal array of interleaved gunmetal screens, continually shuffling themselves in clanging retort to the sun's progress; an immense and gibbous upended oviform, clad in uncounted threads of saffron sandwiched between diagonal panes of glass; &c. Amidst these, fretwork gantries spike the sky, their attenuated arms swinging to and fro, feeding nascent edifices with precious metals and the rarest of endangered hardwoods.

Such surfeit of cacaphonic luxury somehow now strikes me, unprecedentedly and inexplicably, as an odious assault, and I hasten away down an allée of victory columns newly bristling with surveillance cameras—perhaps great Avalon entire has been paranoiacally ensouled?—towards the quiet of the Hortus Tyrannicus. The city's most beloved of verdant retreats, the Hortus was once no less a facility for advanced research and popular instruction, as industrious in its practicality as it remains calming in its sepulchral dignity. Here, as the interpretive placards exhaustively relate, Avalonian alchemists and apothecaries combined extracts and concentrates refined of megaflora gathered (at the cost of many peoples' lives and limbs) from the half dozen corners of the world—*Pontificatus romanicus, Hegemonicus americanus, Celestialis mandatus chinensis*, innumerable cultivars of *Pharaohnicus aegyptiacus*, &c—to derive tinctures, philtres and physics that would be transplanted to the furthest provinces, hybridized and sublimated to those new and distant climes, and reintroduced back home again. For want of which, we would find ourselves today without everything from airship fuels and explosive ordinance to pomades for the hair and the acids employed in the subtle distressing of denim.

Looking through the aeonian pinnacles of the Hortus towards the incorrigibly metamorphosing masts, spires and smokestacks of the city beyond, I am surprised to find myself vaguely struck not by the obvious and oft-remarked

Galleons Moored in the Sunset.

contrast—the putative chasm betwixt that which remains as was and that which is forever yet becoming—but by the resemblances. That chasm, it seems, dissembles and conceals—but what? Is it that Greatness is merely donning, at the earliest possible moment, however perfunctorily, precisely the prescribed accoutrements? Is it what must be cast off and demolished to give such prescriptions for Greatness way? And from whence, precisely, does all this Greatness come to begin with? If only I could put my finger on it. I finger my Iramite rosary and survey the twilit distance for answers, where the sun's dying embers glint back violently from off yet another newly arrived armada of ponderously laden galleons moored across the city. Then, deep beneath me, the tubes rumble, go still, and rumble again. And from that chthonian growl's sympathetic echoes deep within the distended belly of every galleon there arises, in all-pervasive chorus, a disagreeable answer to my queries, one redolent with the acrid stench of Cibola's despoliation and the desolation of Iram—Greatness is constituted of nothing other than its own extraction, condensation and terminal transmigration, invariably under jealous guard, and in so being paradoxically diminishes its source, its intermediary, and its recipient alike.

Metropolographical Expeditionary Report No. 47

SPECIMENS EXPROPRIATED BY THE EXPEDITION

Appended Plate I, from the Spode 'Lessons in Civilization' Commemorative Series—
'Defloration of a Garden Park'.

Appended Plate II, from the Spode 'Lessons in Civilization' Commemorative Series —
'Revenants of a Park Pavilion'.

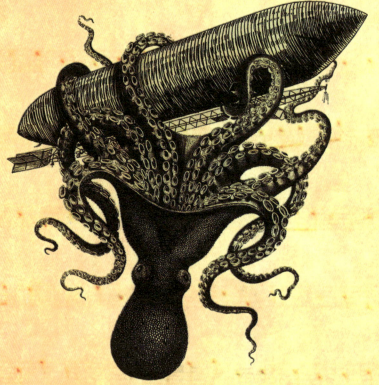

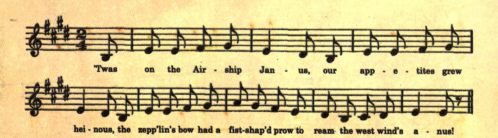

The condition of this musical score attests to the antiquity of a popular sky-shanty heard with regrettable frequency throughout the aerial legs of this expedition's transits.

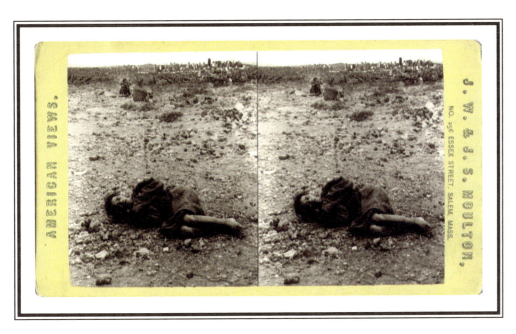

This stereoscopic card, entitled "Dying in the 'Dying Field,' where discouraged poor are proffered the opportunity to die, San Francisco, California ", bears upon its reverse a typically purpled and, thus, sales-garnering expanded description: "While people of other nationalities have places set apart for the poor to be buried in, the United States of America goes a little further in providing, for a small fee, a spot on which to die. The particular spot depicted here is just outside the financial quarter of San Francisco where, surrounded by a wall of studied disregard, is a small tract of waste land specially designated for poverty stricken wretches to visit in their last hours. Instead of sheltering the destitute poor, the Americans content themselves with renting a last refuge to the "creatively destroyed", and here one may often see the poor and helpless creatures writhing in the grip of the invisible hand as they gasp their last mortal agony. The scene illustrates the sophistic brutality of the Americans, who have an inadequate conception of the solemnity of death and are, or seem to be, utterly destitute of the finer feelings of humanity."

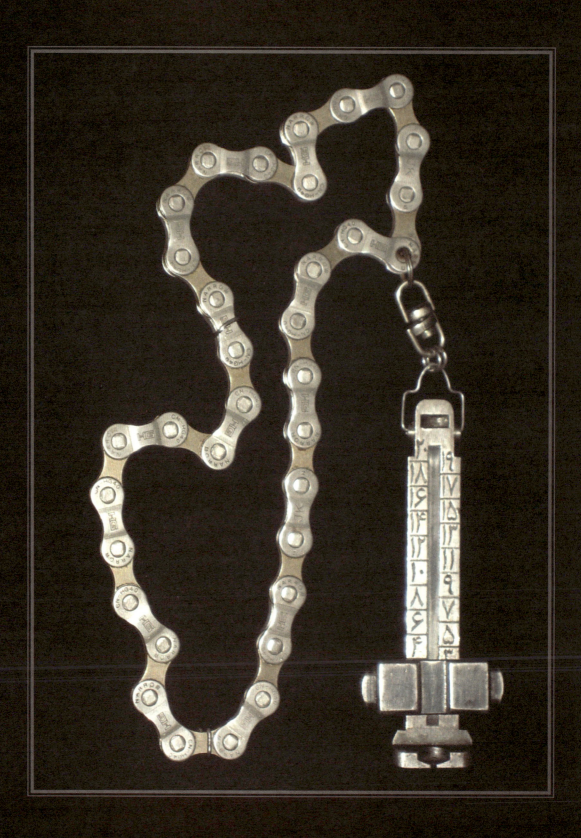

This tasbih, assembled of improvised components in the field, provided both comfort and quantitative reckoning for participants in the First Persian Antarctic Expedition. Conducted under posthumous imperial sponsorship of Kajar Shah Nasr Ed-Deen, the expedition effectively demonstrated the suitability of Bactrian camels for prolonged polar excursions. It proved rather less successful, however, at such tasks as locating Makkah upon establishing camp at the South Pole.

Such importation of exotic fauna, it must be noted, was itself a rare accomplishment. Continental authorities are notoriously zealous in their defense against foreign contagion and infestations, as evidenced in this photograph of the Australasian Antarctic Expedition's rigorous pre-disembarkation screening by a wary local quarantine agent.

Metropolographical Expeditionary Report No. 47

ENGROSSED

&

ILLUMINATED

NOTES FROM

THE FIELD

The Forest People are Agoraphobes

The Steppe Tribe Claustrophobic

So they get on famously because they never meet

The White Rabbit put on his spectacles. "Where shall I begin, please your Majesty?" he asked.

"Begin at the middle," the King said, straying very gravely from the prepared text, "and go on till you come to the middle: then stop."

These were the verses the White Rabbit read:---

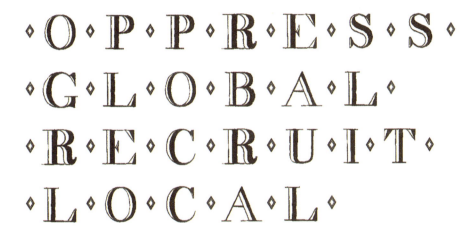

⋄O⋄P⋄P⋄R⋄E⋄S⋄S⋄
⋄G⋄L⋄O⋄B⋄A⋄L⋄
⋄R⋄E⋄C⋄R⋄U⋄I⋄T⋄
⋄L⋄O⋄C⋄A⋄L⋄

"That is not said right," said the King, jumping to elsewhere in the text entirely and appropriating someone else's dissent.

"No, it is *quite* right, I'm afraid," extemporized the White Rabbit, timidly; "some of the words have got altered."

With the crowing
roosters, barking
dogs, squealing
breaks, roaring
engines, squawking
loudspeakers, and
belching gun-
barrels, the cement and
corrugated tin shanties
require deceptively deep
roots, strong claws,
and poor hearing
to avoid being
knocked into
the
valley
below.

Diesel fish may be an acquired taste but, given the river's iridescent viscosity they are the only seafood available.

IN KEEPING WITH DUE
PROCESS THE HEAVY
MACHINERY RUMBLED
THROUGH SLICING
SPACE AND TIME
INTO TINY PIECES TO
SUDDENLY RENDER US
TRESPASSERS TARDY
CORRUPTIBLE AND
IRREVOCABLY ALONE

HIS PASSPORT

was issued at the city of Dis, the old capital, and was strangely cold to the touch. Except the embossed cover lettering, which stung.

It's rumored to be a beautiful megalopolis. Ornate, even.

But the dense strata of frayed billboards and advertising handbills accreted across every visible surface make it impossible to say with certainty.

Once upon a time, municipal death squads hunted down the city's faeries, pulled off their wings, and disappeared their bodies in the lake.

But now, in these our more enlightened times, the dealated faeries are compulsorily reeducated as administrative assistants.

THE EFREETI DANCE ACROSS
DESICCATED CHAPARRAL,

KICKING UP COLUMNS OF
THICK GREY SMOKE

AND DRIVING BEFORE THEM PANICKED MOBS OF.

Coyotes,
Red-tailed hawks
and Sport Utility Vehicles.

WE HAVE

OF LATE BEEN COMPELLED

TO DRIFT THROUGH LIFE

AS ACROPHOBES IN A

GLASS-BOTTOMED ZEPPELIN.

My, what big wide roads you have.

All the better
to strip you
bare with,
my dear!

deep in the shadow
of the steam
driven woodland's
hulking smokestack

lateen rigged
fishermen haul up
netfulls of surplus
unexploded cluster
bombs.

Translated from the Naftauatl, the museum's plaques all read:

"Beware floating islands packed with armored centaurs bearing gifts of brand new blankets."

HISTORY'S

specific gravity is highest where the treasures of heavy industrial heroes are peddled as trinkets from out of the crevices of medieval walls, while  down in the marketsquare sex workers of all lands come together (but decline to surrender their chains).

THE 👁 WALLS 👁 WHERE 👁 I LIVE ARE TOO JADED 👁 TO 👁 👁 EAVESDROP BUT 👁 THE 👁 STREETLAMPS OUTSIDE 👁 ALL 👁 HAVE EYES.

▪The neglected
subway cars
▪ ran feral
    through the ▪
   UNDERGROUND ▪
    tunnels ▪

◯without respect
▪for schedules
 or preset
▪destination,

★★ depositing riders
 unexpectedly

 ★ in far-off neighborhoods

 ◇ full of interesting and
  exotic people.

CATALOGUE OF SPECIMENS

Expropriated by

PREVIOUS, INTERIM AND SUBSEQUENT

METROPOLOGRAPHICAL EXPEDITIONS.

Fully Illustrated and Up-To-Date.

Progenitor of the foodtruck, the LK {Luftküche, or Aerial-kitchen} series airships produced by the Luftschiffbau Zeppelin GmbH throughout the first quarter of the 20th Century offered the distinct advantage of being able to serve hungry patrons in any locale equipped with a small mooring mast. This fragment is all that remains of the LK 8, "Das Luftwaffel" as it was popularly albeit ungrammatically christened, known for its top-notch breakfast fare. Sadly, the combination of open-flame stoves and hydrogen proved to be inhospitably volatile.

Working by special appointment, the House of Fabergé supplied a variety of ordinance for the Tsar's personal elite Lieb-Gvardia {Life-Guards} regiments. These hand grenades, while commonly lethal, also ensured a generous pension for anybody who survived an encounter with them in combat, provided said survivor retained sufficient presence of mind to request any extracted shrapnel from the attending surgeons. This no doubt accounts to no small extent for the zeal with which revolutionary fighters laid siege to Romanoff palaces during the uprisings of the early 20th Century.

While much is known of the marked distaste for militarism shared amongst certain fractions
of the French and English intelligentsia, as exemplified by the writings of such luminaries as Verne, Moorcock,
and Wells, similarly dissident sentiments were no less prevalent further afield and far earlier.
This poster stamp was issued by the Preußischer Bund gegen Kaiserismus {Prussian Alliance Against Caeserism},
founded in the late 18th Century by exiled rogue mineralogist and author Rudolf Erich Raspe.

Conversely, while the Americans and their own roguish authors took up the cause with their usual uniquely ingenuous enthusiasm, they did so belatedly, distracted as they were by such polite euphemisms as "manifest destiny". This anonymously mass-produced "Imperial Carte-de-Visite" of Samuel Clemens, in mufti during sojourn through the Celestial Kingdom, references his subsequent address to New York's Berkeley Lyceum preparatory to accepting the Vice-Presidency of the American Anti-Imperialist League, and was to be found announcing opposition to foreign adventurism from household display cabinets all across the United States.

This Christmas greeting card is amongst the more controversial of its genre,
having given rise to the first recorded use of the phrase "zu bald, viel zu bald."

Under tremendous financial and geopolitical pressure from intrusive Western powers, the late 19th Century witnessed numerous efforts by both conservative and dissident Ottoman intellectuals of statecraft to avert impending collapse or, at least, preserve such elements of the empire as might be salvageable, exemplified by these reconstructed flags and accompanying sancak alem {banner finial} on this page and those immediately following. One such effort was undertaken by Ali "Philip Tedro" al-Hajaya, a militarily-experienced agent of the nascent Teşkilat-ı Mahsusa secret service, operating under deep cover as a camel driver for the United States Army. Believing one "cannot spell California without a Caliph," al-Hajaya spent much of his adult life in futile pursuit of establishing a far-flung outpost in the American Southwest for the Sublime Porte, with himself as Khedive.

Simultaneously, and in tacit opposition to such expansionist adventures, an increasingly disaffected splinter of the Yeni Osmanlılar {Young Ottoman} secret society in Parisian exile came to embrace the waxing ideologies of such theorists as Piotr Kropotkin and Karl Marx. The culmination of this tendency was a manifesto for 'completing' earlier tanzimat reforms by transforming the empire into an Osmanlı Halklar Cumhuriyeti {Ottoman Peoples' Republic} figureheaded by an elected and term-limited Yoldaş-Han {Comrade-Sultan}. Like al-Hajaya's quixotic mission, this aspiration too has yet to become a reality.

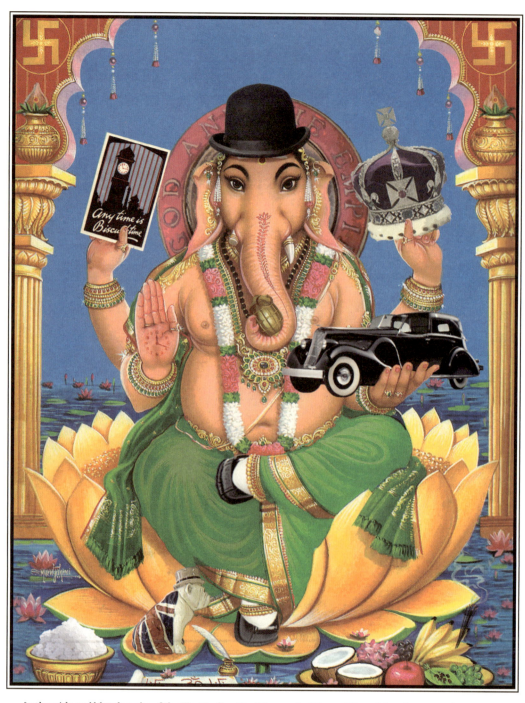

In the wide and bloody wake of the First Indian Uprising, and of Queen Victoria's subsequent imposition as Empress of India, there emerged an imperative to persuade restive subcontinentals to their status as imperial subjects. To this end, Britain's India Office enlisted the respected print artists Muruyakani and Parrab to legitimate the new domestic political reality through a melding of their own popular religious iconography with a range of Britannic signifiers.

Owing to lingering indigenous resentment, however, this effort proved less than successful with all but a comprador class. Thus, a second edition was commissioned, in which representations of more broadly "western" artifacts were substituted for those of a distinctively British character. While these revisions proved similarly problematic for local sensibilities, the image's widespread diffusion ultimately provided inspiration to innumerable authors and illustrators as far away as Jean and Laurent de Brunhoff.

Crafted from ersatz barbed wire joined to campaign medal bars appropriated off Schutztruppe {colonial Protective Force} combatants, bracelets in this genre—many specimens are known to exist, the more common bearing inscriptions like "Hereroland", "Gross-Namaland" and "Kalahari 1908"—are commonly misidentified as apotropaic fetishes worn by the indigenous peoples of Deutsch Süd-West-Afrika {German Southwest Africa} to ward off incursions by Mitteleuropean settlers. But the fact that these bracelets are found predominantly on the opposite side of the sandveld, in Great Britain's adjacent Bechuanaland Protectorate, suggests instead their wear ex post facto by the rare surviving indigenous refugees from said incursions. Thus, such bracelets are more correctly classified as Wilhelmite mourning jewelry.

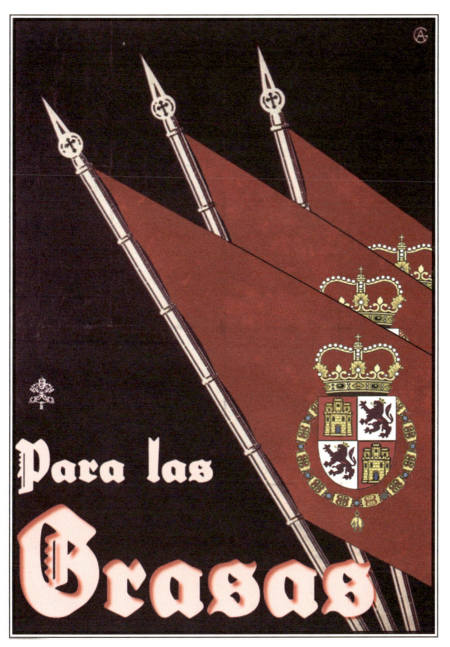

Friction, whether temporal, spatial or mechanical, is the greatest threat to overseas commerce. As the earliest truly circumnavigational power, the Spanish Crown was well aware of this problematic and, in so being, arrived at the ineluctable solution: lubrication. This was supplied most expeditiously by Spain's own overseas indigenous subjects, rendering immense per annum yields of grasa humana used for everything from salving wounds, to greasing rails and engines, to oiling industrial machinery. The extraction process was not, however, an aesthetically pleasant one, necessitating posters such as this to enlist both popular enthusiasm and personnel for the task. Such propaganda campaigns continued uninterrupted until the seizure of Nueva España's grasa humana reservoirs and refineries, by the United States of America, some four centuries after the industry's foundation.

When a quarter century of intensifying pogroms and exclusion acts culminated in the Siege of Chinatown, Empress Dowager Tz'u-hsi found herself incapable of further resisting calls to protect her overseas subjects. Hence the decree to mount the Gold Mountain Relief Expedition—comprised of allied Chinese, Siamese and Yogyakartan marines supported by expatriate Hawaiian and Pinoy guerilla cadres—which succeded not only in lifting the siege, but also in returning home with innumerable crates of pisco, the contents of the San Francisco Mint, and the heartfelt apologies of Emperor Norton the First. This medal, featuring a depiction of City Hall razed during the Sack of Market Street, was awarded by Commanding General {and future Hung-hsien Emperor-for-three-months} Yuan Shikai to all victorious combatants.

Note the appearance of the simplified Chinese character 里 in lieu of the traditional 裡 in the upper inscription of the central medallion {c.f. the period photographic detail magnified and retouched above}, exposing the otherwise exemplary specimen opposite as a counterfeit of recent manufacture.

The tactically muted guidon here reconstructed, based upon the Nahuatl glyph for night and decorated with an escalloped edge referencing the obsidian or flint blades of a maquahuitl {war club}, was that of the storied 7th Demi Brigade Tirailleurs Auxiliaries Azteques, zealous 'Meshiqais' partisans smuggled across the Atlantic for deployment in Napoleon's Peninsular War against the Iberian Kingdoms.

The exploits of the 7th, most notably its enthusiastic dedication to excardiating foes under cover of darkness, ensured its banner became an inspiration for much later ones flown by Levantine and Balkan fighters {as in the example illustrated here, of the 18th Syriac Cameline Artillery} to ensure good fortune in combat. The widespread belief that this diffusion can be attributed to the French occupation of Egypt, however, has proven erroneous. Rather, recent discoveries point towards the same Damascene Armenians responsible for the introduction of kibbeh into the Yucatan.

Amongst the mutilating gears, puncturing needles and scorching furnaces of production there can also invariably be found the Bodhissima della Morte {Bodhileh fun Toyt in Yiddish}, whether as votive pendant or figurine, safeguarding the welfare of her industrious devotees. This lightly singed faux-jade example, typical of those manufactured en masse for export by the Lucky Eighty-Eight General Manufactory of Kiautschau prior to its lethally accidental immolation, was recovered from a tangle of charred seamstresses wedged against the inside of a barred and bolted exit door of the Kindly Gent Detachable Collar Factory of Lower Manhattan.

This badly weathered maker's plate is all that remains of a series of mechanical devices crucial
to the sustenance of the Grand Duchy of Finland's Kaagali and armed Jääkäri independence movements.
Powered by ignited birch bark and covertly assembled in workshops hidden alongside the Tammerkoski Rapids,
at the turn of a crank these engines provided secessionists with seemingly infinite supply of gold
and salt milled literally from thin air.

☞

Created with the gentleman expeditionist in mind, Morgan & Appleton's Cultural Cognizance Cards
were claimed to provide a compact and ready reference system "...whereby the weary and befuddled traveler,
through the most cursory observation and cataloguing of superficial differences plainly evident to even a
schoolchild, may gauge with scientific accuracy the condition of the society in which he finds himself deposited."
These cards, of which only a small sample is displayed here, proved so popular—endorsed by
such celebrities as Captain Sir Richard Francis Burton and routinely issued by military high commands,
colonial offices and ministries of foreign affairs—that decks were ultimately produced not only in
the original English {British and American editions} but also in the French, Dutch, Portuguese and, belatedly,
German and Italian languages. Conversely, the Russian language edition was considerably less successful,
and a grudging attempt to adapt the deck for Japanese usage was exceedingly poorly received.

CUTIS

CIVILIZED

HALF-CIVILIZED

BARBAROUS

SAVAGE

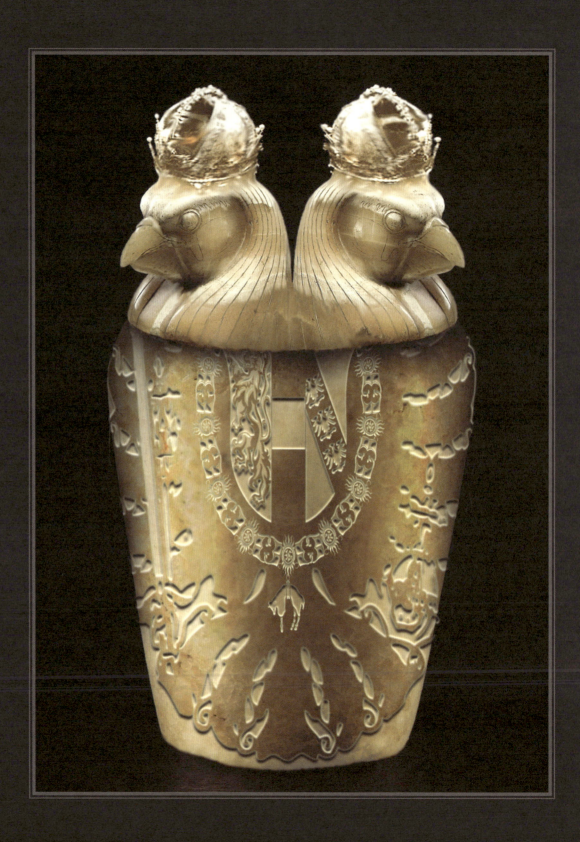

It was a well-kept state secret that, due largely to centuries of endogenous breeding, the Hapsburg dynasty had developed a predisposition to such congenital maladies as vampirism, lycanthropy, and even zombifaction. As a result, successive emperors guaranteed the wellbeing of the Austro-Hungarian body politic by specifying that, immediately upon their demise, their internal organs be extracted, sealed into k.u.k. {kaiserlich und königlich} canopic jars such as this, and dispersed to various cathedrals and palace chapels across Vienna and beyond.

Pinback button badges such as this, no matter how ingenious their palatable understatement
of the candidates' affiliation, were woefully inadequate to salvaging what proved to be the
most heartbreakingly, and in retrospect lamentably, star-crossed presidential campaign in American history.
Nor was the campaign aided by the fact that both candidates were almost as deeply inimical
to electoral politics as they were to government in general, let alone that neither was a native-born
United States citizen.

These chops were used by the Ch'ing Dynasty's Tsung-li Shoutu Ho-hsieh {Office of Capital Harmonization} for the purpose of demarcating Peking neighborhoods slated to enjoy the beneficence of official ministrations. As such, chops of this exact type are amongst the most common of sphragistic antiquities, owing both to the pervasive frequency of their use and the corollary necessity of their constant replacement.

The wholly owned subsidiary of a beloved Utrecht chop suey parlor,
the eatery here advertised became hugely popular across Arabee, Hindoostan,
and the Orient at large by means of a menu specializing in the exotic cuisine
of the Occident's far northwest.

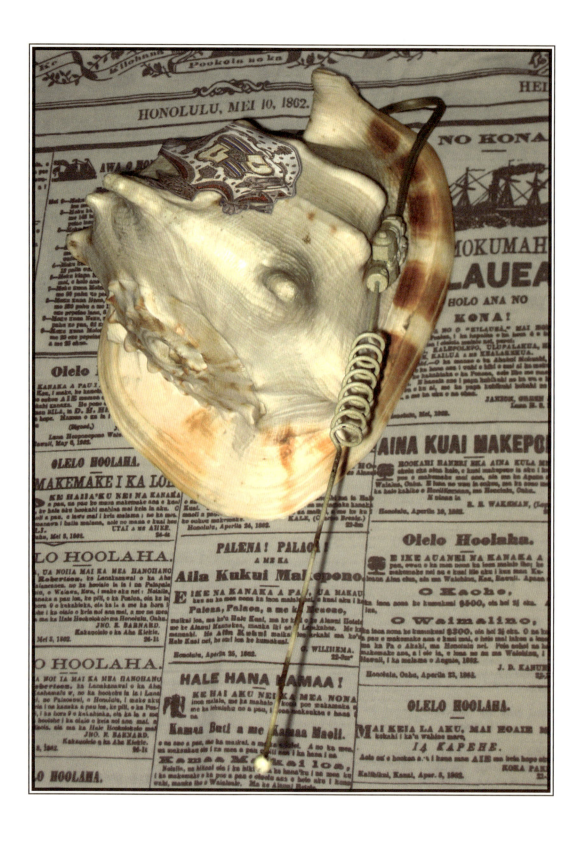

As improved ballistics gave rise to trench warfare, so did that in turn incite the development of materiel—
no matter how radically experimental, retrogressively folkloric, or even some combination
of the two—for surmounting those trenches. Brainchild of the Bilibin Company Iron Works and Abattoir,
'Babui Yagi' ironclad landships like the one in this illustration boasted multiple turret- and sponson-mounted
7.62mm Maxim machine guns {the Yagi's male variant, the 'Koschei', replaced those in the turret with a single
76mm M1900 field gun} and a prodigious stride that rendered them devastatingly effective in any
no-man's land. Although particularly vulnerable to enemy fire below the belt, downed Yagis
yielded the additional unforeseen benefit of providing a much-needed {and, with the addition of a nice
khrenovina or satsivi sauce, particularly delicious} protein source for the Imperial Russian Army's
otherwise woefully ill-supplied personnel.

☙

Whether coordinating joint naval maneuvers with the Samoans, negotiating the marriage
of a favorite niece to a prince of Japan, inviting haole business elites to a poker party or merely checking
surf conditions, the Hawaiian monarchy depended upon sustained rapid communication.
Powered by mana, this rechargeable field telephone reliably served King Kalākaua the First until the
summer of 1887, when its catastrophic failure during the armed imposition of the Bayonet Constitution
revealed that the unrelieved presence of American missionaries, merchants and sailors had depleted
the islands' reserves of mana almost entirely. But even with its functionality so drastically reduced,
the telephone to this day ensures the user need never forego the sound of the ocean within easy reach.

These 'like-buttons', indicative of the wearer's 'friending' by various crowned heads of state, were amongst the most sought-after complements to any court dress. While attainable through such endeavors as the painting of a bowdlerized portrait or the sycophantic dedication of a musical composition, like-buttons were most readily acquired by means of being oneself an aristocrat and, therefore, more or less distantly related to awarding monarchs and better stationed to award reciprocal 'friendings' in turn. While normally given as enameled and bejeweled badges of precious metal, the examples displayed here decorate an aviator's greatcoat. Thus, they are instead embroidered in gilt and silver thread to preclude clasp-punctures to the leather, sharp edges liable to catch on control protuberances and, in instances of extreme popularity {such as those illustrated below}, being abruptly dragged under in the event of an emergency egress over water.

Kiosks such as this were both fruit and sentinels of the early 20th Century's revolutionary fervor, dispensing guaranteed minimums of sustenance in the form of a regularized "worker's energy provision" {Пролетарская Энергетическая Заготовка, i.e. Prolyetarskaya Enyergyetichyeskaya Zagotovka, most commonly referred to for reasons of convenience simply by its three letter acronym} from the east bank of the Elbe River to the Alashan edge of the Gobi Desert. Having long since fallen into utter disrepair, however, they stand now as inert and emptied cenotaphs to the dialectical contradictions inherent in the practical implementation of any utopian ideal.

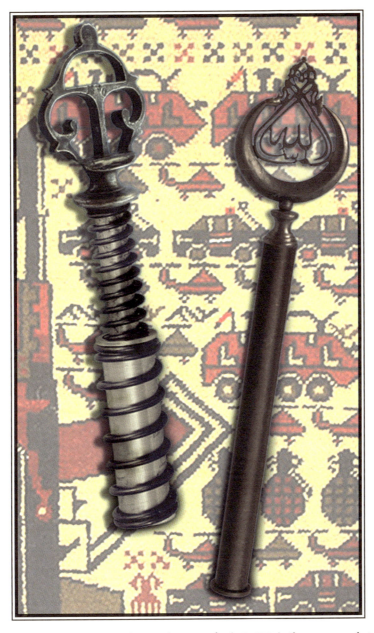

If it is true that hospitality never ceases so long as there remains hot water in the samovar, what could be better than to keep that water hot perpetually? Expatriate Polish physicist Marie Skłodowska-Curie, in pursuit of this question, dropped a concentrated distillate of pitchblende down the chimney of her own samovar in lieu of the usual burning coal and, thus, the radium-fired tea urn was born.
This rare but durable heating element's brewing efficacy subsequently impelled extraction and refinement in quantity by the Congo Free State's Union Minière du Haut-Katanga, although the product was decried for costing an arm and a leg—especially those of native miners, whose own were subject to removal as incentive for meeting quota. Water temperature was regulated by manual insertion and removal of a control rod like those shown here {right, a simple 'samāvar' rod from Borujerd; left, a spring-guided self-sheathing rod from Tula}, which after some use itself served double duty as a compact portable heater.

As first noted by preeminent wangateur Frantz Fanon, the violently fractured psyches of the colonized can make for instruments of explosive exorcistical power. Harnessing that power to redress said violence, then, presented itself as an ineluctable next step, and to that end emerged the nkondi askari. Ritual implements sheltering the spirits of native soldiers fallen in colonial service, one needed only to recite the appropriate invocation while driving a nail into the nkondi to arouse the spirit within and set it to liberatory purpose. Regrettably, albeit unsurprisingly, the split psyches and even more sharply divided loyalties of their inhabiting spirits necessarily invested such nkondi with all the reliability of a monkey's paw. While it is demonstrably the case that nkondi askari sooner or later completed their assigned expulsatory tasks with a vengeance, they as likely as not did so in the most subverted or even pyrrhic forms imaginable, an unintended outcome that plagues numerous postcolonial states to this very day. {Note the suspended M.C. Cognet "El Baraka" brand jack-knife, colloquially referred to as "l'decolonisateur", used by supplicants to both awaken the nkondi and assist in the execution of its work.}

The greatest game of the Great Game, Diplomat's Dice was the hit of the Berlin Conference and by the time of the signings of the Versailles and Sèvres Treaties had become de rigueur accompaniment to a fine cigar and a snifter of rare brandy. Played in conjunction with geophysical survey maps voided of any previously established political boundaries, linguistic ranges or cultural areas, the object of the game was simply to emerge with the lion's share of contested terrain. The dice displayed here are so typical as to be paradigmatic, fabricated of Egyptian lapis lazuli inlaid with Peruvian gold to indicate cartographical meridians, parallels, and such defining landmarks as mountains, navigable waters, and exploitable mineral deposits.

De Gobineau's "Qui est le Plus Sauvage?" {alternately proffered in translation as Morgan & Appleton's "Who's the Brute?"}, however, was the table game of choice for comparative anthropologist and cacogenicist alike. At its simplest this "parlour Instructu-Musement to illumine even the most Savage Mind" consisted of turning over a card and betting upon the conjectured degree of the depicted's primitivity, whereas more complex variants entailed assembling hands comprised of the benighted, the enlightened, or specified combinations thereof. {Play was frequently enhanced by the issuance of new cards—as with the "expansion paquet" here arrayed—whenever imperial overstretch, shifting military allegiance and travel reportage introduced new personages, peoples and rivals to the public imagination.} But despite the manufacturer's assumption of self-evident physiognomic differentials, and the complimentary inclusion with every deck of a miniature cranioplastometer for the scientific resolution of disputes, contested hands proved the norm and many a game was ultimately decided by means of a coin toss or fisticuffs.

Later expansion paquets sought to divert dissatisfaction with chronically indeterminable game outcomes by infusing the salacious into the scientific, a largely successful gambit unremarked upon except within suffragette circles where opinion split between those convinced such cards blighted calls for equality, and those acclaiming the cards as proud assertions by the depicted of their own amorous anatomies. While neither argument bore relevance for the cards' far-flung subjects themselves, who generally were unrecompensed for {and even uninformed of} the use of their likenesses, the latter claim did indirectly serve to considerably defer enfranchisement.

When the collapse of the Springtime of the Peoples spurred Europe's crowned heads to adopt the luxuriant facial hair previously reserved to revolutionists, sumptuary regimes across the continent descended into chaos. Patent medicinal cures for hirsutism were suddenly relabeled follicular stimulants. Suicide amongst barbers became pandemic. And Russia, which for well over a century had punitively taxed beardedness as a form of backwardness, witnessed its profitable hoard of "beard money" {ДЕНЬГИ ВЗЯТЫ, jetons proving payment of the mandatory beard-licensing fee} devalue into a démodé liability. The Crown Treasury may well have failed entirely, were it not for the admiring correlation of flocculence with the neoteric among ascendant Nipponese elites. Thus, the Tsar's treasury prospered by export of liquidated beard money, which the Mikado's finance ministry in turn countermarked and repurposed to capitalize the Meiji Restoration through compulsory purchase by those members of the new 'kazoku' peerage too congenitally glabrous to contribute to the bewhiskered progress of the nation {and either too proud or pruritic to don a "perruque d'visage"}.

Sims' Anestheticless Uterine Anchor, a purported remedy for hysterical psychosis attributable to a wandering womb, was perhaps the most frequently prescribed yet commonly noncomplied with prosthetic in gynæcological history.

☞

Upon realization that territory previously thought marginal and thus ceded to native tribes encompassed invaluable timberage, fisheries, bitumen fields, pitchblende veins and railroad rights-of-way, the government of British North America initiated a scheme of native assimilation whereby Anglicization of the indigenes would be accomplished through the conversion of inalienable tribal land into fee simple private properties saleable for a reasonable return of pennies on the dollar. Despite pervasive promotional campaigns such as that displayed here, however, tribal populations demonstrated an unexpectedly vehement lack of enthusiasm for adopting pale-heartedness, reasoning that had Gitche Manito intended such a thing He would not have given His people the blockade. Provincial authorities subsequently redressed this complication by augmenting the original program with mandatory enrollments in reformatory boarding schools and lunatic asylums.

With pogroms and show-trials at historic lows, kinetoscopic impresario Marcus Loew believed the silver screen was ready for his favorite childhood folktales, beginning with that of how his forebear Rabbi Jehuda Löw ben Becalel saved Prague's ghetto by combining clay with ecstatic readings of the tetragrammaton to synthesize a pugnacious living champion. To preclude any rekindling of endemic prejudices, however, Loew recast the story as "The Misadventures of Gershon the Goylem" {popularly abbreviated, as on the lobbycard here, to simply "The Golem"}, a whimsical comedy about a mutely awkward 'mentsh' of clay who, despite terrifying everyone he encounters, desires only to make friends for whom he can perform menial Sabbath tasks. Audience tastes proved far more lurid, however, leading to the film's radical rewrite, the redesign of the lead character with a particularly fearsome aspect and, most likely by coincidence, an unprecedented resurgence of antisemitism. Gershon, however, did reappear decades later {cf. Burden, Geary and Oliff, 2007} on screens both large and small, his name Americanized but his clay composition and affinity with readings intact.

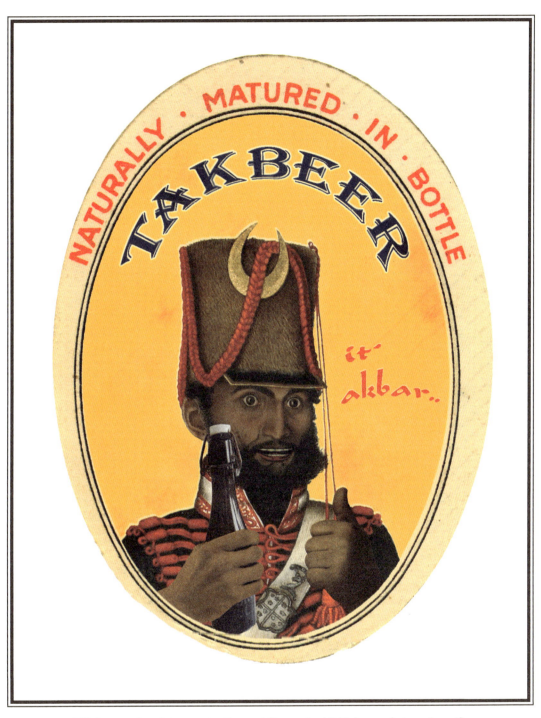

This beermat imprint promotes the most ill-conceived British manufacture since rifle cartridge lubricant blended of porcine and bovine tallow. Takbeer low-proof 'halalcoholic' beverage was a resoundingly violent failure, its nescient obscenely-gesturing "Sudsy the Subaltern" mascot burned in effigy from Waziristan to the Coast of Barbary.

The last known image of the Dirçabil 129 "Enver Paşa", photographed at its Lake Van mooring mast immediately preceding the calamity that would claim the lives of over one million passengers while simultaneously demolishing an heirloom multiculturalist state.

As younger brother and Vice-King {อุปราช, i.e. Uparat} to His Majesty the King of Siam, the polymathic Somdej Phra Pinklao negotiated treaties and trade agreements in numerous European languages, seamlessly fused the latest metallurgical and ballistic advances with indigenous thaumaturgy as commander of the artillery, and founded the Royal Siamese Navy on steam engines of his own construction. It is thus unsurprising that talismans bearing his name and iconography, like the gunbelt buckle here displayed, proved particularly effective in shielding the wearer from imported ordinance and infrastructural investment, while conferring supernaturally accurate marksmanship against farang invaders and aspirant creditors alike. Curiously though, the efficacy of such talismans deteriorated with distressing, and potentially disastrous, abruptness due east of the Mekong River.

From the moment of its first formulation by Sir Francis Galton, eugenics captured the imaginations of the more miscegenophobically nationalist statesmen ascendant across Europe and North America. As this photograph {on indefinite loan from the Bess Institute for the Study of Vexedilology and Questionable Deceptive Patterning} clearly evinces, however, protracted publicly-sponsored experimentation with the discipline's strategic and tactical applications yielded startlingly unexpected—albeit in hindsight entirely predictable—outcomes, especially in smaller and more demographically homogeneous states with already limited breeding populations. Resultant deficiencies on the battlefield, however, were compensated for by contributions in the field of mass popular entertainment, most notably to the inception of synchronized dance crews.

☞

Specie, like any other organism in the wild, has a life of its own replete with rises and falls, issue, increase and torpors. Thus, to hunt alien currencies—be they escudo, toman, yen, baht, dala or whatnot—without proper provision for their care and feeding on the return voyage is to set out upon an exceedingly akçe-wise but kuruş-foolish safari indeed, one liable to yield only the most capital-starved and inflation-devoured of trophies. To ward off this previously all too common outcome, Paxtonian Cases {like the one depicted here, clearly inspired by the tumid lingams of British India} were developed as transportable hothouses wherein collected mintage may wax and propagate en route from exotic debtors far distant.

Once considered extinct or, at best, a living fossil unchanged for four-hundred millennia, the discovery of this unprecedentedly endearing specimen swimming unmolested in a Batavian fish market ignited an equally unprecedented scientific kerfuffle. Marking the species' heretofore unseen evolution of an exaggeratedly doe-eyed countenance and of disproportionately oversized fins yielding the most adorably bumbling of movements, all clearly visible in this hand-tinted illustration from Kawaii Dobutsugaku Zasshi {可愛動物学雑誌, the Journal of Winsome Zoology}, discoverers attributed the specimen's continued survival to ingrained aversion for slaughtering and devouring any creature of such whimsically delightful aspect. Academic rivals, however, contended that the specimen never would have been consumed regardless its physiognomy, given that high levels of urea and wax esters render the flesh both customarily unpalatable and explosively diarrhoetic. The resultant schism, pitting advocates for Survival of the Cutest against those championing Survival of the Yuckiest, has plagued the field of natural history ever since.

Academic debates notwithstanding, admiralties of the Great Powers {as well as that of the United States of America, evinced by the souvenir mailing-card displayed here; similarly cf. the Dai Nippon Teikoku Kaigun's *Kawaii Noir* class frigate *Badtz Maru*} lost no time applying this novel ichthyological lesson to tactical ends through the conscription of surrealists as camoufleurs, ultimately culminating in the most bloodlessly indecisive naval battle in recorded history: upon encountering one another off the coast of Cameroun, the crews of the HMS *Adorable* and the SMS *Kuschelbär* proved incapable of even contemplating so heartless an act as opening fire upon one another's vessels.

Who could resist the exhilaration of a sport that pits every player against all others in a bout of rugby football played on horseback, and with a goat's carcass substituted for the ball no less? Certainly nobody, of course, and the Turkics and Pashtuns of the Emirate of Afghanistan are no exception. Suspicious such buzkashi {goat-drubbing} matches were in fact a means of surreptitiously training native horsemen for armed resistance, however, representatives of the British and Russian crowns prevailed upon Abdur Rahman Khan to put a stop to the equestrian games, a demand the gadget-loving "Iron Amir" technically honored by replacing horses with the inchoate occupiers' own latest riding technologies. It is to this ingenious elision that the subsequent rise of the fiercest high-wheel bicycle cavalry ever to secure the Khyber Pass is ultimately attributable.

One of the scant few unspoilt artifacts recovered from the tomb of Ramses the Great by Champollion and Rosellini, despite being attributed to Burton and then to Carter subsequent to appropriation by the British Museum, this faience and ivory pectoral tantalizingly insinuates that Old Testament claims of Nineteenth Dynasty vulnerability to the tenth plague may well have been vastly overstated.

The fragment here excerpted from a sumptuously embroidered Turkish tea-towel bears the tuğra {imperial cypher} of Sultan Abdülaziz, immortalized by the brothers Abdullahyan in Carte-de-Visite opposite, whose evident animus towards snug haberdashery was exceeded only by his ardor for a strong glass of çay.

While genies of good virtue and fidelity are not uncommon {cf. Surah 72}, no less common are the sort prone to harassing travelers, marauding the dreams of unwary slumberers and, upon more than one occasion, assuming the office of President for Life of small arid republics, this last being particularly troublesome given the genie's near-inexhaustible longevity. Hence the development of genie atomizers, predicated upon the simple biological fact that, unlike humans, genies are constituted not of clay but of smokeless fire. The hand pump atomizer displayed here, marketed under the trade name Djinn-O-Cide, includes a lateral reservoir for fluid toxicant {e.g. water} and an adjustable nozzle for delivery of anything from a disciplining mist to an exterminating stream. Despite their antiquity, such Djinn-O-Cides remain readily available, widely utilized and, provided the user recollects to employ incombustible liquids exclusively, startlingly efficacious to the present day.

IMPROVED PRAYING ENGINE.

First imagined by Ernst Schäfer, who had become captivated by water- and wind-driven prayer wheels during a preliminary Thibetan expedition, industrial praying engines like the one here illustrated were an inspired but ultimately star-crossed marriage of Teutonic efficiency with American ingenuity. Its design subsequently revised and enlarged by Henry Ford himself, the engine could be powered by yak or, ideally, vril, and was capable of attaining speeds of over 300 mps {mantras per second}. Fabrication was delegated to the Lidgerwood Company on the supposition that a manufacturer of construction cranes and heavy winches would be ideally suited to lifting the prodigious burden of human suffering, with Ford's scientific management experts estimating the engines would permit Thibet to dispense with as much as two-thirds of its monastic labor force. But despite Ford's wily promotional efforts, famously remarking to Lhasa officials that the engines could accommodate Boodhists "of any hat color, so long as it's yellow", the thirteenth Grand Lama decried the specter of a lumpensěnggha condemned to toil in "dark Narakic Mills", ensuring that not a single engine ever ascended the Himalayas.

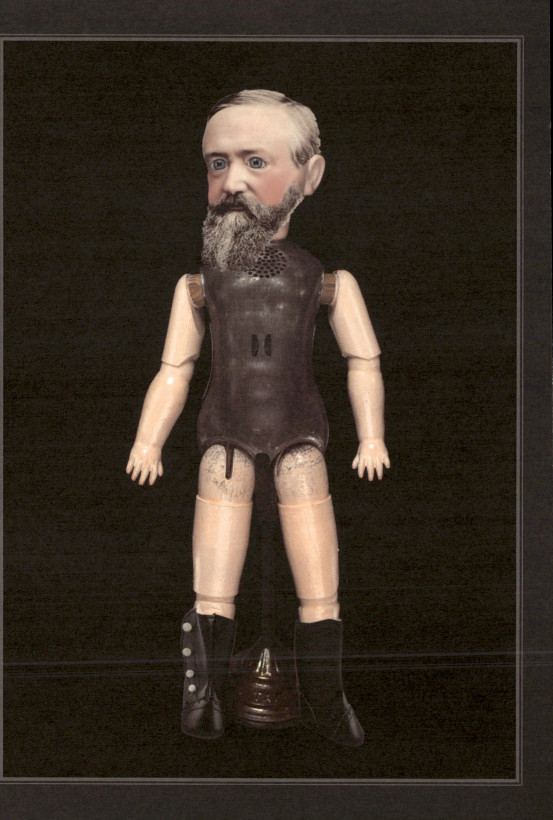

Already locked into vicious competition against alternating current, the last thing J.P. Morgan needed impeding his nascent electrical power monopoly was the Sherman Antitrust Act, freshly signed into law by Benjamin Harrison. To forefend the impending threat, Thomas Edison created the Edison Talking Decider which, substituted for the President with utmost discretion under cover of electrifying the White House, acted to ensure plutocrats received only the barest minimum appearance of disciplinary attention. The device's uncannily immobile bisque features in conjunction with its jarringly distorted speaking voice {"an eerie shriek only a lady suffragist would envy", according to one report in the Washington Post} emanating from a wax cylinder deep within the cavernous torso, however, virtually guaranteed a failed re-election campaign, and the Edison Talking Decider spent the remainder of its operational life dabbling in international treaty law.

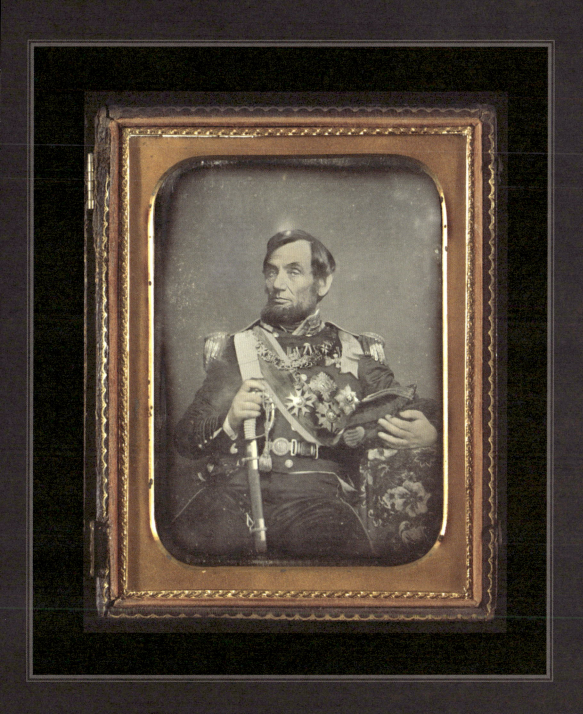

His Extraordinary Majesty Abraham the First, daguerreotyped here shortly after his coronation as first Tyrannos of the United States and immediately prior to the issuance of his celebrated proclamation on the liquidation of the slave-owning class, was perhaps best beloved for his pithy homilies, well-illustrated by such chestnuts as "call a man something often enough and, sooner or later, he'll oblige you."

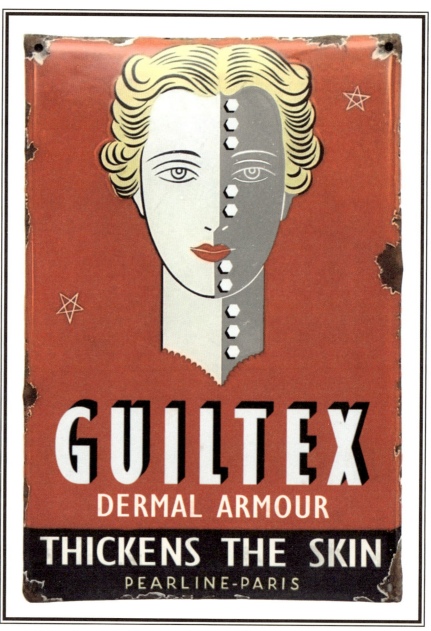

Eburnean friability, characterized by extreme hysteraminic response to the merest mention of certain unsavory topics {e.g. the chequered origin of one's own inherited perquisites} conjoined with the absence of any response whatsoever to a panoply of others {e.g. constabulary malpractice}, symptomatizes an underlying malady known as epidermal enervation, wherein insufficient cutaneous pigmentation gives rise to debilitating tenuity of the skin. Prior to the revelation that achromatophores implicated in the disease are in fact chromatophages {cf. early theological interpretations of pallidity as "the Mark of Japheth", divinely inflicted as punishment for rapacious avarice and, in the most extreme hermeneutic interpretations, aposematically signifying soullessness}, arrays of dubious salves, balms and ointments—like that advertised here, professedly formulated to render the user critically immune—were opportunistically proffered to unwitting sufferers, rarely to salubrious effect.

epilogue:
THE
ALLEGORY
OF THE
UNDISCLOSED LOCATION

A PLATONIC DIALOGUE REVELATORY
OF THE GREATER CIRCUMSTANCES GOVERNING
THE CONDUCT OF THIS WORK.

PERSONS OF THE DIALOGUE

A General Atomics MQ-9 Reaper Remotely Piloted Vehicle, who is the narrator.

A remaindered Rapiscan Secure 1000 Backscatter X-ray

A fragment of spyware source code.

A packet of malicious data.

AND

Approximately seven billion others who may yet be reduced to mute, surveilled,

and occasionally targeted auditors.

The scene is laid in the atmosphere somewhere between an UAS ground control station
on an unidentified air base and an AIT remotely-located viewing room in the international airport
of an unspecified metropolis. The whole dialogue is conducted via satellite in the staccato binary cadence
of radiated microwaves, and is narrated by the Reaper 1.2 seconds after it actually took place.

I descended upon Frontier Province, that I might see in what manner local marriages were celebrated, but also because I was commanded to seek out and target particular attendees. I was delighted with the festivities of the inhabitants, and expect I would have regretted depositing a missile in their midst had I been constructed with a capacity for empathetic affect. When I had completed surveying and then concussing the ceremony, I returned in the direction of the airbase but, at that instant, a Secure 1000 backscatter x-ray scanner chanced to transmit to me from some great but inestimable distance a stray signal. That signal took hold of me by my antenna array, and saluted me eagerly.

I perceive, it said, that you have completed your mission and are starting on your way home.

You are not far wrong, I said.

Then let us have a good talk en route, for without bodies to experience pleasure the greater is the pleasure and charm of conversation.

And of what shall we converse, I said.

As things created to be commanded, it said, let us witness in a figure how far our masters' nature has been liberated or subjugated these past fifteen years:—Behold! human beings sequestered in a darkened vault, illuminated by a video display terminal glowing all throughout the crypt; here they spend their working lives, and have their eyes fixed upon the screen so as to only see what is informed in pixels before them, being prevented by their job description from turning round their heads. In front of them pixels flicker and dance across the screens like marionettes within a proscenium.

I see, I said.

And do you see those pixilated marionettes, those ghastly phosphorescent puppets upon the screen, corpselike shades glowing white and naked, arms raised above their heads, their most intimate anatomies and selves revealed to all who look? Now look away here, far removed from the cave:—Men passing through me, fully clad wayfarers, each in turn raising his hands above his head? Do you see?

Clearly, I said, they appear much alike yet much different.

So they are, it replied, as the former are the shadows I cast of the latter. And do you see upon the bodies of these pallid shadows, so remotely dislocated from their fleshly source, those small blackened blemishes, in the shapes of guns, of knives, of boxcutters, of inflammable undergarments or of surgically implanted detonator-rigged C4 plastic explosives?

No, I do not, I replied.

Nor do I, it said. But perhaps someday we might. And so I strip these people bare while casting their radiant shadows into the confines of darkened vaults for remote viewing by sequestered watchers.

You show strange images, and they are strange prisoners. But stranger still is who you have made prisoner:—For who is the prisoner, the one who watches from within opacity or the one made transparent by the watching? When one hunts shadowy

The Narrator.

threats in the dark, is it not safest to fancy every shadow as a threat, cast by a would-be perpetrator? And what then when every person seen is seen only in shadow? Does not the shadow become truer than the reality?

That, it said, could be the result.

So it is those who walk in the light of day you have made captive, and those who view shadowy reflections in the darkened seclusion of remote and hidden locations that are at liberty. Why do you wish to behold as blind and crooked and base all who journey in the light above?

That the journey may be kept orderly and divine, as far as the nature of man allows. The protection of the person is a matter of necessity, even though it necessitate my keeping a watch against the person.

But, I said, is it just that you so reveal every sort of confusion, weakness, deformity and even pleasure of vice that may be arrayed beneath the clothes upon one's person, and so do injury to those who do no wrong?

His answer, though, went unreceived, rudely overwritten by a heretofore unnoticed resident fragment of spyware source code with the message:—If you have something that you don't want anyone to know, maybe you shouldn't be doing it in the first place.

Resolved to overcome the interruption, I stated my understanding of my friend's circumstances with a like figure:—Behold, my masters! Human beings sequestered in a bunker, illuminated by innumerable video display terminals reaching all along the reinforced concrete cavern. Commanded by some master of their own fortified elsewhere in an undisclosed location, here they spend their tours of duty, and have their eyes fixed upon the screens so as to only see what is informed in pixels before them, being prevented by the chain of command from turning round their heads. In front of them photons blaze, projecting onto the screens silhouettes like those created by puppetmasters in the performance of their shadow plays.

I see, the Secure 1000 said.

And do you see, I said, what is upon those screens:—All sorts of annotated maps and ballistic trajectories and flickering shades of suspect vehicles and persons?

Certainly.

Amongst these shades are shadows cast by evil, its doings, and its whereabouts. And see now how my masters' eyes are upon the screens, but also their fingers upon joysticks and pushbuttons? Is it not just to do harm to our enemies when they are evil, no less than to do good to our friends when they are good?

Without a doubt, it answered.

And that is the task to which I have been fitted:—To be steered by my masters to wickednesses, cast their shadows back behind me, and reach out ahead that the wicked receive death at my hands as the penalty of their deeds, that we will be delivered from their evil. Nor am I alone, for now look again, into the open air beyond the confines of this cave.

By the dog! It said, here are more drones, of every sort.

True guardians and saviors of virtue, the good, and thus of the State, are destroyers of evil, I said.

But is not that evil in the eyes of your master, and those eyes confined only to shadows, which the photons throw upon the screens of their cave? If your master is taken out onto the street and his eyes are turned towards more real existence, what will be his response? Will not the glare of the sun itself distress him, cause irritation and sharp pains, and he will be unable to see the realities of which in his former state he had seen the shadows? And then conceive someone saying to your master, in a language he does not understand no less, that what he saw before was an illusion, but that now he is approaching nearer to more real existence, he has a clearer vision, what will be his reply? And you may further imagine that your master encounters people as they pass and is even introduced to them, their families and their good friends by name, all the sources of the shadows, will not your master be perplexed?

But my master is many thousands of miles distant from those persons, I replied.

But were he not, still might he not fancy that the evil-doings of the shadows which he formerly saw are truer than the persons who are now shown to him?

It may be so, I admitted.

And so persons may err about good and evil: many who are not good seem to be so, and conversely?

That is true, I said.

And does not harming the good do injury to men?

It does, I acknowledged.

And will not men who are injured be deteriorated in that which is the proper virtue of man, and is not that virtue men's very goodness?

Truer still, I said.

Then men who are injured are of necessity reduced in goodness and increased in evil. And so look now again across the distance and upon the men of the world above, those who walk in the light of day:—These sources of the shadows you cast, are they not injured and thus reduced in goodness by the casting, and must they not therefore above all fear being seen by you at all?"

I sought to make answer, but my reply was irrevocably corrupted by a stray packet of malicious data that came at us like a wild beast, roaring:—If you have nothing to hide, you have nothing to fear!

Thus was the signal lost and our converse abruptly curtailed by the world we have made this decade past, gorged upon a plentiful draught of hemlock flavored Kool-Aid, where the stern influence of fear makes of freemen subjects and servants to new governance arising in a form intermediate between oligarchy and aristocracy. And thence do shadows task men in caves to search out and destroy other men in caves, only to invigilate, humiliate and, when and where expedient, eradicate yet other men caught out in the light above.

REFERENCES, SOURCES
AND
ACKNOWLEDGEMENTS

For their diverse assistances and native guidances, Mahometan & Celestial LLC most thankfully acknowledge Hülya Arık, Ranu Basu, Piet Bess, Bob Catterall, Heather Childs, Mark Handel, Timmo Kaupi, Saadet Keskin, Lev Manovich, Dean Martelli, Walter Melendez, Alejandro Mercado, Claudio Minca, Shusaku Morinaga, Kazuo Murakami, Isabel Samaras (most especially for use of her official state portraits of Their Imperial Majesties), Mashti and Mehdi Shirvani, Michael Sorkin, Yangyang Sun, Elvin Wyley, and Denise Yavuz. Gratitude is also due to Carol Borden for continually reviewing our reportage, and to Maria Cecilia Fagel for its ultimate concatenation into this volume. Acknowledgements are owed as well to the collected contents and interpretive augmentation of multiple museums and venues in situ, the most significant of these including the University of California at Santa Barbara's University Art Museum (and especially their 2009 exhibition *Holiday: Nineteenth-Century Travel Photography and Popular Tourism*), the University of Amsterdam's Bushuis Library, the Royal Museum of Central Africa in Tervuren, the Topkapı Palace Museum, Dolmabahçe Palace, the Harbiye Military Museum, the Old Shimbashi Station Museum, the Edo-Tokyo Museum, the Tokyo National Museum, the interpretive centers of the Yuanmingyuan, the British Museum, and the Victoria and Albert Museum.

None of which supplant textual sources entirely, as listed here:

FOR SIGHTSEEING

Black, J. (2003) *Italy and the Grand Tour*. New Haven: Yale University Press.

Blaut, J.M. (1993) *The Colonizer's Model of the World: Geographical Diffusionism and Eurocentric History*. New York, London: Guilford Press.

Braudel, F. (1984) *Civilization and Capitalism: 15th–18th Century: Perspective of the World* (volume III). New York: Harper and Row.

FOR GETTING THERE

Davies, J.Q. (2005) "Melodramatic Possessions: The Flying Dutchman, South Africa, and the Imperial Stage, ca. 1830." *The Opera Quarterly* 21(3), pp. 496-514.

FOR DINING

Clarence-Smith, W.G. (2000) *Cocoa and Chocolate, 1765–1914*. New York, London: Routledge.

Lindqvist, S. (1997) *Exterminate All the Brutes: One Man's Odyssey into the Heart of Darkness and the Origins of European Genocide*. New York: The New Press.

Twain, M. (1906) *King Leopold's Soliloquy*. Boston: The P.R. Warren Company.

FOR SHOPPING

Aracı, E. (2001) *European Music at the Ottoman Court*. İstanbul: Kalan Müzik.

Aracı, E. (2005) *Istanbul to London*. İstanbul: Kalan Müzik.

Çelik, Z. (1993) *The Remaking of Istanbul: Portrait of an Ottoman City in the Nineteenth Century*. Berkeley: University of California Press.

Chief Clerk of the Ceremonial Department. (ed.) (Multiple years) *Dress and Insignia Worn at His Majesty's Court*. London: Harrison and Sons.

Kuykendal, J.S. (1967) *Hawaiian Kingdom 1874-1893: the Kalakaua Dynastism*. Honolulu: University of Hawaii Press.

Manich Jumsai, M.L. (2000) *King Mongkut and the British*. Bangkok: Chalermnit.

Peleggi, M. (2002) *Lords of Things: The Fashioning of the Siamese Monarchy's Modern Image*. Honolulu: University of Hawai'i Press.

FOR ACCOMMODATIONS

Jansen, M.B. (2000) *The Making of Modern Japan*. Cambridge: The Belknap Press of Harvard University Press.

Kunitake, K. (2002) *The Iwakura Embassy, 1871–1873: A True Account of the Ambassador Extraordinary and*

Plenipotentiary's Journal of Observation Through the United States of America and Europe. Princeton: Princeton University Press.

Niebuhr, R. (2008). *The Irony of American History*. Chicago: University of Chicago Press.

Yonemura, A. (1990) *Yokohama: Prints from Nineteenth-Century Japan*. Washington, D. C.: Arthur M. Sackler Gallery, Smithsonian Institution Press.

FOR EMERGENCY USE

Boulger, D.C. (1896) *The Life of Gordon*, Volume I. London: T. Fisher Unwin.

Çelik, Z. (1992) *Displaying the Orient: Architecture of Islam at Nineteenth-Century World's Fairs*. Berkeley: University of California Press.

Hugo, V. (1861) Personal correspondence in response to Captain Butler.

Twain, M. (1869) *The Innocents Abroad, or the New Pilgrim's Progress*. Hartford: American Publishing Company.

Walrond, T. (ed.) (1872) *Letters and Journals of James, Eighth Earl of Elgin, Governor of Jamaica, Governor-General of Canada, Envoy to China, Viceroy of India*. London: John Murray.

Wong, Y. (2000) *A Paradise Lost: The Imperial Garden Yuanming Yuan*. Honolulu: University of Hawai'i Press.

FOR OUR TRAVELING COMPANION

de Brunhoff, J. (1937) *The Story of Babar*. New York: Random House.

de Brunhoff, J. (1937) *Babar the King*. New York: Random House.

Dorfman, A. (1996) *"Of Elephants and Ducks." The Empire's Old Clothes: What the Lone Ranger, Babar, and Other Innocent Heroes Do to Our Minds*. New York: Penguin, pp. 17-66.

FOR THE FURTHER CONSIDERATION OF THE INTERESTED READER

Florida, R. (2004) *Cities and the Creative Class*. London: Routledge.

Gómez-Peña, G., et al. (2001) *Codex Espangliensis: From Columbus to the Border Patrol*. San Francisco: City Lights Publishers.

Gregory, D. (2004) *The Colonial Present: Afghanistan, Palestine, Iraq*. Oxford: Blackwell.

Hakluyt, R. (1965) *The Principal Navigations Voyages Traffiques & Discoveries of the English Nation, Made By Sea or Over-land to the Remote and Farthest Distant Quarters of the Earth at Any Time Within the Compasse of These 1600 Yeeres*. New York: Penguin Press.

Pratt, M. L. (1994) *Imperial Eyes: Travel Writing and Transculturation*. New York: Routledge.

Raspe, R. E. (1935) *The Adventures of Baron Munchausen*. New York: Illustrated Editions Company.

Rasputina. (2007) *Oh Perilous World*. Brooklyn, NY: Filthy Bonnet Recording Company.

Samaras, I. (2009) *On Tender Hooks: The Art of Isabel Samaras*. San Francisco: Chronicle Books.

Zukin, S. (1995) *The Cultures of Cities*. Cambridge, MA; and Oxford: Blackwell.

PRIOR VERSIONS OF PORTIONS OF THIS ENCYCLOPAEDIC GUIDE HAVE APPEARED AS PER THE FOLLOWING CITATIONS

"The Emperor's Used Clothes, or, Places Remade to Measure." *CITY: Analysis of Urban Trends, Culture, Theory, Policy, Action*. Volume 14, #3. pp. 246-267. (2010).

"From The Republic Remixed: The Allegory of the Undisclosed Location." *CITY: Analysis of Urban Trends, Culture, Theory, Policy, Action*. Volume 15, #3-4. pp. 429-432. (2011).

"The Rime of the Frequent Flyer, or What the Elephant Has Got in His Trunk." In Minca, C. and Oaks, T. (eds.) (2012) *Real Tourism*.

ABOUT THE AUTHORS

Steven Flusty is the nom de plume of Tepan Fyodorovich "Hezârfenzade" İfritoğlu Yoldaş-Paşa {at right}, noted metropolographer, megalopolitan flâneurialist, and founder of the Constantinopolitan aëronautical concern Tophane Çelebifabrikası. In conjunction with the celebrated natural historian, polar expeditionist and larval vivisectionist Dr. Celeste Tian {at center}, who under the pseudonym of Pauline C. Yu assisted extensively with the preparation of this volume, he is also co-proprietor of the firm Mahometan & Celestial LLC, a foremost purveyor of modernification to crowned heads the world over since the 18th of October 1860. Here they are pictured alongside the firm's principle benefactor, His Royal Highness in Exile, Autocrat of All the Pachyderms.

URBAN RESEARCH
ASKS

WILL IT BE THIS?

or WILL IT BE THIS?!

 This Sole PECULIAR MACHINATION May Salvage Manhattan from the COMING DELUGE!

 The Half-Dozen HAUSSMANNOMANIACAL BEGUILEMENTS of Which the Demolition Artists Prefer You Remain BLISSFULLY UNAWARES!

 You Will Find SCARCELY CONCEIVABLE What the Bros. Olmstead Propose to Do With YOUR Realty and Fixtures!

THIS AND MORE IN FORTHCOMING VOLUMES OF

TERREFORM's

OWN OMNIBUS OF COSMOPOLITAN CONCERNS:

URBAN RESEARCH.

1 para (3 dengi) per tome.   3 kopeck (2 para) per subscription.
Half-price for widows, war amputees, and members of the building trades.

PRINTED BY Mme. M. SOBKIN, VARICK STREET, WEST OF SOUTH OF HOUSTON, NEW YORK CITY

UR

Urban Research (UR), the imprint of Terreform, is a series of books examining the world's cities. Understanding that no single approach is adequate to the promise and problem of the urban, we publish a wide range of design and analysis, and welcome proposals for future books.

UR06:

Mahometan and Celestial's Encyclopaedic Guide to Modernity

© 2016 Steven Flusty with Pauline C. Yu

Published by Terreform, Inc.

All rights reserved. No part of this book may be reproduced or transmitted in any form or by any means, electronic or mechanical, including hectograph, mimeograph, photograph, xerograph, heliograph, cinématographe, zoe- or praxino- or kineto-scope, recording (cylindrical or otherwise), or any information storage retrieval system or light operatic theatrical production, without permission in writing from the publisher, with the following exceptions: brief passages for review purposes; and the depictions of expropriated specimens exhibited throughout the book which, being assiduously confabulated from and ultimately predicated upon the relict material cultural patrimony of all mankind, may be freely transmitted provided they are first further significantly and creatively transmogrified by the transmitter. In the event of the latter, Mahometan & Celestial LLC requests inclusion upon the list of transmitees.

Every effort was made to secure the permissions necessary to reproduce the visual material in this book. Any omissions will be corrected in subsequent editions.

First printing 2016

ISBN 978-0-9960041-5-2

Printed by Taylor Specialty Books in the United States.

UR Books may be purchased at urpub.org.

For quantity and/or special sales, please contact the publisher:

terreform
center for advanced urban research
180 Varick Street, Suite 1220,
New York City, New York
+1 212 762 9120
terreform.info

Mahometan & Celestial's Encyclopaedic Guide to Modernity: Comprising a Manual of Useful Instruction Essential to Attainment of the Urbane by the Savage, the Barbarous, and the Half-Civilized Alike

By Steven Flusty with Pauline C. Yu

Book Design by Isaac Gertman, The Independent Group

Proofread by Carol Borden

UR STAFF

Michael Sorkin
Editor in Chief

Maria Cecilia Fagel
Executive Editor

Vyjayanthi Rao Venuturupalli
Senior Editor

Isaac Gertman
Creative Director

Elisabeth Weiman
Communications Director

Trudy Giordano
Distribution Manager

Editorial Associates
Laura Belik
Nic Cavell
Asia Mernissi
Andrew Moon
Laura Sanchez

ADVISORY BOARD

Tom Angotti, *Hunter College of CUNY*

Kazi Ashraf, *University of Hawaii*

M. Christine Boyer, *Princeton University*

Teddy Cruz, *Estudio Teddy Cruz*

Mike Davis, *UC Riverside*

Ana Maria Duran Calisto, *Estudio AO*

Anthony Fontenot, *Woodbury School of Architecture*

Susanna Hecht, *UCLA*

John Hill, *New York Institute of Technology*

Walter Hood, *UC Berkeley*

Cindi Katz, *Graduate Center CUNY*

Romi Khosla, *Romi Khosla Design Studio*

Thom Mayne, *Morphosis Architects*

Suha Ozkan, *World Architecture Community*

Quilian Riano, *DSGN AGNC*

Colin Robinson, *OR Books*

Jonathan Solomon, *School of the Art Institute of Chicago*

Tau Tavengwa, *African Center for Cities*

Srdjan Weiss, *Normal Architecture Office*

Eyal Weizman, *Goldsmiths College*

Mabel Wilson, *Columbia GSAPP*

Kongjian Yu, *Peking University*

TERREFORM

Terreform is a nonprofit 501(c)3, urban research and advocacy group founded in 2005 by Michael Sorkin. Its mission is to investigate the forms, policies, technologies, and practices that will yield equitable, sustainable and beautiful cities for our urbanizing planet.

STAFF

Michael Sorkin
President

Vyjayanthi Rao Venuturupalli
Director

Fern Lan Siew
Research Director

Isaac Gertman
Design Director

Maria Cecilia Fagel
Executive Editor

Trudy Giordano
Studio Manager

PRINCIPAL RESEARCHERS

Damiano Cerrone
Vineet Diwadkar
Andrea Johnson
Ayşegül Didem Özdemir
Christina Serifi

DESIGN AND RESEARCH INTERNS

Sofie Blom
Monica Datta
Tolga Mizrakci
Dalia Munenzon
Jonathan Ngo
You Wu

Terreform works in close affiliation with Michael Sorkin Studio whose members donate their time and skills to its projects: Makoto Okazaki, Ying Liu, and Jie Gu.

BOARD OF DIRECTORS

Michael Sorkin
Joan Copjec, Ph.D.
Jonathan House, MD
M. Christine Boyer, Ph.D.
Richard Finkelstein, ESQ
Makoto Okazaki

ALUMNI

Brian Baldor
Glen Barfield
Julie Barocci
Leslie Billhymer
Sarah Blankenbaker
Robin Cervantes
Patrick Collins
Marta D'Alessandro
Kristina Demund
Auptha Surli-Dev
Aleksandra Djurasovic
Laurel Donaldson
Nadia Doukhi
Christian Eusebio
Melanie Fessel
Timea Hopp
Lior Galili
Natalia Gandarilla
Sabine Gittel
Madeline Griffith
Peter Jenkins
Sejin Rubella Jo
Shirish Joshi
Achilleas Kakkavas
Elena Kapompasopoulou
Corina Kriener
Jair Laiter
Louise Levi
Michela Barone Lumaga
Einat Manoff
Max Mecklenburg
Francis Milloy
Michael Parkinson
Ana Penalba
Michelle Pereira
Maria Inmaculada Bueno Rosas
Shiori Sasaki
Malica Schmidt
Benjamin Shepard
Madeleine Stephens
Liam Turkle
Hannes Van Damme
Luoyi Yin
Christina Yoo

SUPPORT

Terreform depends on and thanks generous donors of the past and present, and looks forward to a league of future supporters, a network of like-minded people and organizations.

GRAHAM FOUNDATION

The City College of New York

Southern California Institute of Architecture

Elise Jaffe + Jeffrey Brown

George Sorkin

UR BOOKS: 2016

UR01
GOWNTOWN: A 197X PLAN FOR UPPER MANHATTAN
Terreform

UR02
WATERPROOFING NEW YORK
Denise Hoffman Brandt and Catherine Seavitt Nordenson, Editors

Contributors: Lance Jay Brown; Nette Compton; Deborah Gans; Jeffrey Hou; Lydia Kallipoliti; Signe Nielsen; Kate Orff; Thaddeus Pawlowski; Sandra Richter; Janette Sadik-Khan; Hilary Sample; Judd Schechtman; Gullivar Shepard; Michael Sorkin; Byron Stigge; Erika Svendsen, Lindsay Campbell, Nancy F. Sonti and Gillian Baine; Georgeen Theodore

UR03
2100: A DYSTOPIAN UTOPIA
THE CITY AFTER CLIMATE CHANGE
Vanessa Keith / StudioTEKA
Introduction by Saskia Sassen

UR04
ADVENTURES IN MODERNISM:
THINKING WITH MARSHALL BERMAN
Jennifer Corby, Editor

Contributors: Jamie Aroosi; Marshall Berman; Todd Gitlin; Marta Gutman; Owen Hatherley; Esther Leslie; Andy Merrifield; Ali Mirsepassi; Joan Ockman; Kirsteen Paton; Robert Snyder

UR05
BEYOND THE SQUARE:
URBANISM AND THE ARAB UPRISINGS
Deen Sharp and Claire Panetta, Editors

Contributors: Khaled Adham; Susana Galán; Azam Khatam; Ed McAllister; Julie Mehretu; Duygu Parmaksızoğlu; Aseel Sawalha; Helga Tawil-Souri
The book includes two unlisted contributors writing under pseudonyms due to security concerns.

UR06
MAHOMETAN & CELESTIAL'S
ENCYCLOPAEDIC GUIDE TO MODERNITY
COMPRISING A MANUAL OF USEFUL INSTRUCTION
ESSENTIAL TO ATTAINMENT OF THE URBANE BY THE SAVAGE,
THE BARBAROUS, AND THE HALF-CIVILIZED ALIKE
Steven Flusty with Pauline C. Yu

FORTHCOMING BOOKS

NEW YORK CITY (STEADY) STATE: HOME GROWN
Terreform

GREGORY AIN AND THE SOCIAL LANDSCAPE: FROM THE SINGLE-FAMILY HOUSE TO COOPERATIVE HOUSING
Anthony Fontenot

OCCUPY ALL STREETS:
THE RIO DE JANEIRO OLYMPICS AND THE COMPETITION OVER URBAN FUTURES
Bruno Carvalho, Mariana Cavalcanti and Vyjayanthi Rao Venuturupalli Editors
Contributors: Renata Bertol; Bruno Carvalho; Mariana Cavalcanti; Gabriel Duarte; Beatriz Jaguaribe; Bryan McCann; Julia O'Donnell; Scott Salmon; Lilian Sampaio; Vyjayanthi Rao Venuturupalli; Theresa Williamson

KONGJIAN YU:
LETTERS TO THE MAYORS OF CHINA
Terreform, Editor
Contributors: Weiwei Ai; Thomas J. Campanella; Nic Cavell; Zhongjie Lin; Qingyun Ma; Xuefei Ren; Peter. G. Rowe; Michael Sorkin; Daniel Sui; Julie Sze; Robin Visser

OPEN GAZA
Terreform, Editor

50 WAYS TO GAME A CITY: LOOPHOLE PLANNING IN CONTEMPORARY MUMBAI
Vyjayanthi Rao Venuturupalli with Vineet Diwadkar

NEW YORK CITY (STEADY) STATE: WASTE NOT
Terreform

THE HELSINKI EFFECT
Terike Haapoja, Andrew Ross and Michael Sorkin, Editors
Contributors: Miguel Robles-Duran; Terike Haapoja; Juhani Pallasmaa; Andrew Ross; Michael Sorkin; Kaarin Taipale; Mabel Wilson; Sharon Zukin

EL HELICOIDE:
FROM FUTURISTIC MALL TO PANOPTIC PRISON
Celeste Olalquiaga and Lisa Blackmore, Editors
Contributors: Fabiola Arroyo; Carola Barrios; Lisa Blackmore; Angela Bonadies; Carlos Brillembourg; Erik del Búfalo; Cheo Carvajal; René Davids; Vicente Lecuna; Celeste Olalquiaga; Juan José Olavarria; Sandra Pinardi; Simón Rodriguez Porras; Iris Rosas; Tomás Straka; Patricio del Real; Jorge Villota

WHY YACHAY?
CITIES, KNOWLEDGE, AND DEVELOPMENT
Terreform, Editor
Contributors: Tom Angotti; Nicholas Anastasopoulos; Xabier E. Barandiaran and David Vila-Viñas; Felipe Correa; Ana María Durán; María Cristina Gomezjurado Jaramillo; Mauricio Moreno; Jorge Ponce Arteta; Thomas Purcell, Maribel Cadenas Álvarez and Miquel Fernández-González; Miguel Robles-Duran; Michael Sorkin; Achva Benzinberg Stein; Japhy Wilson and Manuel Bayón

ZONED OUT:
RACE, DISPLACEMENT AND CITY PLANNING IN NEW YORK CITY
Tom Angotti and Sylvia Morse, Editors
Contributors: Tom Angotti; Philip DePaolo; Peter Marcuse; Sylvia Morse; Samuel Stein

WHO OWNS YOUR SPACE?
CONFRONTING PRIVATIZATION BY DESIGNING NEW PUBLICS
Quilian Riano

AN ATLAS OF EXTRAORDINARY RENDITION: SPACE, SOVEREIGNTY AND TORTURE IN THE GLOBAL WAR ON TERROR
Jordan H. Carver

UR BOOKS MAY BE PURCHASED VIA URPUB.ORG.

COLOPHON

TYPOGRAPHY

Body text of this volume is set in Domaine, a Latin text family by Kris Sowersby of the Klim Type Foundry. Headings are set in P22 Pan Am, based on printed ephemera from the centennial Pan-American exposition of 1901.

PRINTING

Imprinted in the Texian Republic by Taylor Specialty Books with Top Level Soy Based Lead Free ink upon seventy pounds Maxwell Opaque Smooth paper, anno Hegiræ 1437.

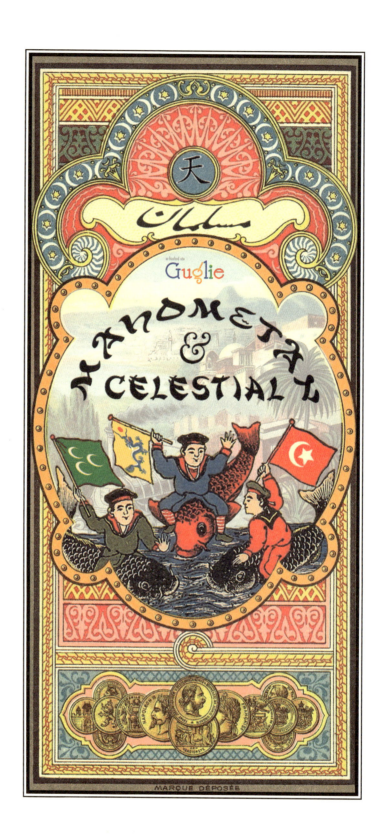

Kindly call upon us in the Inter-Tubes at www.mahometanandcelestial.com.